From
Leeds to
Lashburn

From Leeds to Lashburn

Enjoy Joyce S

Joyce

Sjogren

FROM LEEDS TO LASBURN

Copyright © Joyce Sjogren, 2023

Published by Joyce Sjogren, Edmonton, Canada

ISBN:
    Paperback   978-1-77354-504-2
        ebook   978-1-77354-505-9

Publication assistance and digital printing in Canada by

PUBLISHING
PageMaster.ca

Thanks To:

Jay Branch (Regina), Lori Feldberg and Isabel Didriksen (Wetaskiwin), my sister Marjorie Leitch, The Lashburn Museum, The Edmonton Sun re Bull Trains and Red River Carts taken from the Canadian Best Selling Series – *Alberta in the 20th Century* and the Internet for helping me.

Disclaimer

James Whiteley came to Western Canada in 1903 and Louise Hemsley came a year later to what is now called Lashburn, Saskatchewan from Leed's England. I have written the story surrounding their time in Western Canada by remembering some of the stories she told me and doing some research. Some of the dates and events may not be accurate. I have recreated it the best I can.

Dedication

To my children and grandchildren who are
direct descendants of the Whiteley's, Donald
Sharpe jr. (Dylan); Linda & Doug Barry
(Morgan & Joscelyne); Peter & Susan
Sharpe (Brandon & Breanne)

Contents

Prologue 1

Chapter One 3

   Leeds, England 3
   The Letter 10
   The Trip 13

Chapter Two 17

   Winnipeg 17
   The Trek West 19

Chapter Three 27

Chapter Four 37

   Destination Lashburn ... 37

Chapter Five 61

   The Bannisters 67
   The Soddy 70

Chapter Six 81

Chapter Seven 95

   The Move 97
   Doctor Arrives 104

Chapter Eight 115

   Christmas 115
   Spring 119
   Spring Planting 127

Chapter Nine 129

   Weddings 129
   Fall 137
   Thanksgiving 139

Chapter Ten 149

   Christmas 156

Chapter Eleven 167

   The Pageant 167
   Christmas 169
   The Baby 186

Chapter Twelve 191

   Moving To Lashburn ... 191

Chapter Thirteen ... 217

   Harvest 217
   Baby Florence Arrives .. 231

Chapter Fourteen ... 243

   Hospital Visit 243

Chapter Fifteen 257

   The Girls 257

Epilogue 263

Prologue

My story starts in Leeds, England, an industrial city, where Louise was born and raised and where she would learn the many talents that sustained her and her husband through the rough times. James, her husband, was also from Leeds, a devout member of the Church of England. Through hard work and adaptability, they survived the harshness of the land and raised two daughters. Both lived a long life, more comfortable in the last few years, always remaining solidly behind the teachings of the Bible.

In my story I have navigated around stories that Louise, whom I met in 1958 when I married her grandson, Donald Irving Sharpe(son of Elizabeth 'Betty' & Albert Irving Sharpe), often spoke of regarding the times surrounding her time in Saskatchewan. She mentioned the Railroad, the Province and Rev. Lloyd(the city of Lloydminster is named after) during the 1900's when she made the determination to immigrate and meet up with her true love. She persevered through all the difficulties

coming to the bald prairie, knowing very little of the multitude
of facets of climate and farm life always remaining deeply devout.

There were many times after gleaning from my memory, I
had to research it to learn the truth about the living quarters
and arrangements. Sometimes, I used excerpts from newspaper
clippings and information from the Lashburn Museum and the
internet.

Rev. Barr was well known to the government for enticing
immigrants to a land of milk and honey. That land often took its
toll. Some managed to return to their homeland, disappointed
and suffering, and some could not. They had used all their hard
earned money to start a new life, only to find they were not suited
or could not sustain themselves.

Chapter One

Leeds, England

The whir of the Singer sewing machines and the odd hum or word drowned out the street noises as Louise Hemsley sewed at Leed's Sewing Factory, worrying and fretting about her future. All the girls were married at her age and here she was twenty years old, unmarried, living at home, under her mother's watchful eye.

Every so often she stopped and fingered the telegram in her pocket. It had come to the factory office and she wondered why? There seemed such an urgency in it. It read,

"Please come Stop I need you Stop Sent letter Stop, James Whiteley," dated May 15, 1903.

She wanted to cry or scream while her heart started racing. She could hardly get her breath pondering the depth of the tele, while staring at her sewing machine.

There were nights that she had spent thinking he would never come back and that she would never see him again, often crying into her pillow. He was handsome in her eyes, with his longish face and deep blue eyes fringed with dark lashes. It was the way he always greeted her that made her whole body tingle. She was so in love.

It was nearly a year since she had heard anything from him and three years since they had met at church. Trying to concentrate on her sewing was impossible, she couldn't help but relive the scene in the church. He used to sit across from her and periodically took a quick look making her blush. When she fidgeted her mother would nudge her and Jimmy, her brother would close his eyes and giggle waiting for a motherly slap on his knee. Father always seemed amused by this display.

My father was a slight man, about an inch taller than mother, with a thin face, and prominent ears which we always teased him about. His hair was fine and short with grey appearing at the sides making him look dapper. Smiling to herself, she thought about the many times she cut his hair.

Then she thought about her mother who was short, not really fat but more solid with black hair swept into a bun at the back of her head. She pictured her now at home concentrating on her sewing while giving commands. She often showed little humor, pursing her lips when disagreed with.

Louise closed her eyes and looked down at her sewing, but failed to get going. Her mind wandered back to the church, where James had sought her out and how every Sunday they managed to get together and talk. Oh how she missed him and so did young Jimmy, her curly haired brother, who was only 12. Jimmy was the one that pestered mother until she finally gave in and invited James to Sunday dinner. That's when James discovered that she played the piano and told them how he liked that and how he liked playing the trombone at church. Her mother seemed pleased about this musical aspect of him. When James got bold enough to ask her out to a young people's meeting, she was almost afraid to ask her parents because somehow her mother had always interfered. However, this time she found the courage and her father intervened telling her mother that Louise was old enough to make up her own mind.

"You always take her side," her mother had replied, but left the decision up to Louise.

She was glad her father had stood up for her, because when it came to mother, she would have given in. Thinking about her, she quietly said, "my mother, forgive me, is of a strong demanding character." When the coworkers turned to look at her, she realized she had said it aloud so she stood up and went to the loo.

Her co-workers had grown fond of this quiet, wholesome, curly haired, young woman, with the peaches and cream complexion, who never spoke a bad word about anyone.

"Did Louise say what was in the tele?" a nasal voice asked.

"Leave her alone, you don't understand," replied Beth, Louise's best friend, who worked beside her.

"Yeah, what was in that tele she got this morn? Betcha, it was from her dear boyfriend? Maybe he found himself another woman, uh?"

"It is none of your business, leave it," came another reply.

A hum of approval came from the other girls, just as Louise re-entered the room. She was still thinking about James and how they had been inseparable often walking hand in hand when no was looking. She didn't care who saw, but he did.

Then she thought about the stranger who had suddenly appeared at one of their church meetings. A man, in his fifties, short, heavy set with an unruly mop of brown hair and piercing brown eyes. He maintained he was a minister from Canada and preached in a booming voice about young people coming to a new land where there were so many opportunities. He went on and on about it, explaining that it was virgin land that promised crops like you have never seen before. A world of milk and honey. All this talk got to James, who got caught up in the excitement about unclaimed land, finally announcing to Louise that he was thinking about immigrating. It sounded so good and really what was there to keep him here. There was little work in this smelly place. The Boer War was over and soldiers were returning home making jobs even more scarce. She could still hear him teasing her about missing the sounds of horses, the smell of coal fires, people hawking, the hours you have to work, and your mother nagging at you all the time. He told her that they would start their own life in a new country. It would be wonderful, Louie. I love you and want you to marry me in the new country he had said. It had almost been too much for Louise but she realized she would do anything just to be with him which started her thinking about immigrating too.

Within a month, he had signed up and scraped enough money to pay for his passage and some for food and equipment. He put $10.00 down to reserve some land in the British colony. Louise had promised him faithfully, that she would follow him to the ends of the earth if necessary. When she quietly informed her parents one evening the information had been too much for her mother and she had taken to her bed for a week.

She could still hear her father's words that evening, when he took her aside and spoke softly, 'My dear girl, as much as I hate to see you leave, I believe you must. You have my blessing and prayers. We love you so much. Your mother will understand one day. She has relied on you too much through the years. She never gives you time to yourself and you were always at her beck and call. I realize this now and it breaks my heart. I should have stood up to her many years ago.' He continued to reassure her telling her that he would make sure she had the money and not to worry, kissing her on the cheek. He added that they would get word to James through the church that she was coming. She could still smell the new leather from the shop and visualize his head bent over a shoe where she had often helped him out. She loved the old shop with its worn front step and smattering of shoes all around and always the wonderful smell of leather. There she always felt at ease, with no one to nag at her or tell her to hurry. So often she was tired running her mother's errands, only to be asked to do more work at home. Realizing she was still sitting looking into space, she fingered the tele again and decided to stand and tell them what she was planning.

"If you must know, my boyfriend wants me to come to Canada, and that is what I shall do."

All at once, the girls around her jumped up and were hugging and wishing her well and when one girl started to cry, they all did until a voice commanded they get back to work.

"It's tears of happiness we have, sir," said a small girl from the back of the room. "We're happy for Louise, and it's her we're gonna miss."

Suddenly it did not matter that the place was so drab, the windows small and dusty as was everything in the city. In spite of all that, Louise felt satisfied that she kept her sewing machine clean and shiny for she constantly cleaned the bits and pieces of thread from her table and washed her hands frequently. She was beginning to get excited thinking she must plan when the bell rang to end the day's work.

All of a sudden there were sounds of voices and hurrying feet all heading home for the evening tea. Taking her time, she waited for Beth, so they could walk home together. Beth was such a tiny person, full of zest and sometimes impish, with sparkling dark eyes and such a big heart. Louise felt like a big sister towards her and they felt safer walking together. The two girls, stepped outside the factory, into the noisy street. Louise glanced around as if seeing it for the first time. How cold it looked. Maybe it was time to move on, but teared up thinking about leaving home.

"I've been talking to you for at least two minutes. You haven't heard a word, I said?" stated Beth, still walking beside Louise.

"Sorry, Beth, my mind is going round and round."

"I'm excited for you. Imagine everything will be new and different. I would leave this dump in a minute, if I had the chance."

"I can't even imagine what it is like over there, how far away it seems," answered Louise.

"Treat it like a trip to the unknown, and remember I want you to write often."

"I haven't had a letter from James, to tell me what to do and where to go," she answered with a worried look.

"Oh, James will write. I can sense it."

"I must stop and see father. See you tomorrow." she called as she waved to her friend and boarded her own train.

On board, she settled down in a seat, still thinking about how she was going to tell her mother about the tele. She continued to think about James, oblivious to the people around her. He loved her she knew, but hadn't even kissed her. Of course, she had wanted to, but was too shy to make the first move. She fingered the tele again to reassure herself. Shaking her head, she hurried to get off as the lights of her station came into view. Quickly jumping down, she adjusted her coat and rushed to her father's shop at the end of the street. Her father, wasn't expecting her today, but, oh how she needed his support.

"Hello, father," she called as she took off her coat. When she called again she saw him just hanging up his coat.

"Oh hello daughter, I've had to stay home today. Your mother was in a bad way again." he called.

"What is the matter?" she asked, but before, he could answer, she said quietly,

"I got a tele at the factory," drawing the paper from her pocket.

"Did he ask you to come?" and when she didn't reply, he added, "You are going to Canada, aren't you? You have had no letter from James, have you?" he spoke as he automatically picked up a shoe to shine.

"No, but the tele, says, sent letter."

Puzzled, he stopped and looked at her. "I wonder," he said and then added, "Finish up and we will go home early."

"Mother?" she queried, but he did not answer.

The Letter

They locked up and walked out into the fresh misty air. It was a short, pleasant jaunt home with her father, but he was not talkative tonight.

At home, her father opened the door quietly and both slipped off their coats. Louise hurried to the kitchen to put the kettle on for tea, while her father disappeared in search of her mother. The stove was cold, dishes from breakfast were still on the table which made Louise wonder where her mother was until she noticed a note on the counter. She called to her father that mother had left a note saying she had gone to measure for some dresses and would be back later. Louise went to see what he was up to and found him upstairs in their bedroom opening and closing drawers.

"What are you looking for father?"

"I believe your mother has been keeping a letter from you. but I can't find one."

After thinking a moment, she darted downstairs into the living room where her mother's sewing machine was. Fumbling with the sewing machine drawer, a letter fell out as she pulled it open.

"Oh," she said. It was addressed to her. She showed the letter to her father and disappeared into her bedroom.

While he was having his tea, Louise came and sat down beside him tears streaming down her face. "How could mother?" was all she said, showing him the letter. It was short, on a piece of yellowed paper that read,

"My dear Louie, I miss you so much. Will you please come and marry me? I need you so. I can make arrangements on this end. It is in Western Canada, east of a place called Saskatoon, near a place called Wirral in the British colony. You will have to make the journey from Winnipeg by Red River Cart train. They stop here on the way to Saskatoon. You can stay at a rooming house, some miles from us. Remember this is wild country, so be strong, my darling.

Love James."

"It is a cruel thing to do, and she must apologize to you. I thought she was sick today, but I believe now that it was guilt that kept her in bed."

Just then the door opened, and a demanding voice called, "I'm home, just in time for my tea." When she looked at the two sitting at the table, she knew at once that they were on to her. Instead of sitting down with them, she proceeded to go to the living room and her sewing machine, but her father called her back.

"You have done a cruel thing in keeping that letter from Louise.'

"I, uh, just don't want Louise to go that's all."

"That is her decision, not yours."

"I'll take my tea in my bedroom."

"You will take your tea right here. From now on, we are not waiting on you." and with that he stomped out of the room, still agitated. Her mother never moved. She wasn't used to being talked to like that. Her father was always so calm and quiet. It didn't matter, Louise knew she would go. Then she thought of her brother, Jimmy? How is he going to cope? She loved him dearly.

Later, she took a walk, thinking all the time about her move. *'I will have to make plans for my voyage. I will have to ask father to help me plan my trip. What shall I take? How much money will I need? Oh, there were so many questions. She needed to talk to Beth about clothes. Perhaps she would invite her for the weekend. That way they could plan together. It would be fun.'*

The next few weeks flew by. Her father had found another trunk for her in addition to the one in the attic. Along with Beth, she had chosen some of the clothes she would need making sure they were not overly fancy. Excitement was giving Louise some sleepless nights worrying about every little thing. Her mother was starting to realize she could not rely on her, but Louise continued to make tea and bake and clean. Once her passage had been assured, between her father and her, they talked about what she would need for food and incidentals. Her mother was adamant about adding some desiccated soups in her luggage, although Louise was against it. The company had indicated that they were giving her a heavy duty sewing machine as a parting gift, for what she had no idea. Her father insisted on adding thread, needles and some other small parts and her hair scissors, which, for the life of her, she wondered why.

In church, Louise was approached by the minister. He had been talking to her father and had made provisions for Louise to spend a few days in Winnipeg, Manitoba, Canada, with a resident minister and his wife, who would give her some insight into her journey. She agreed for her father's sake even though she was confused.

Her last day at work was a difficult day. She enjoyed the sewing, and kept a meticulous station, and the company realized it. She would not miss the drab streets and the train trip home every day, but she would miss stopping at the shoe shop to visit with her father. He was the one she was going to miss the most as well as her little brother who was a pest, but she loved him. He cried and wanted to come with her vowing to come to Canada as soon as he could. She cried with him. They were very close, right from the time her mother gave birth to him. A lot of the babysitting was left to Louise while her mother worked with one sewing project or another. He was a normal, active boy. Now, perhaps her mother would pay more attention to him. *God works in mysterious ways.* And with that she immediately stood up and said a teary goodbye to her co-workers.

The Trip

In a few days, she would be embarking on her journey. She had chosen a long fitted dark brown coat with a fur collar and a tam to match. Her mother had embroidered a rose on one side of her tam, in bright pink, that Louise wasn't quite sure of, but perhaps it was her mother's way of saying 'goodbye'. Of course, her father gave her a pair of sturdy shoes. Her dress was plain cream colored, fitted at the waist, with a long skirt and long sleeves.

Getting ready to leave, Jimmy thought she looked quite the lady. Her Mother said nothing but clung to her for several minutes. Louise couldn't help the tears as she took one last look at her mother, the house and surroundings. It would be tucked in her book of memories forever.

Father took her to the station, bound for Liverpool, and paid for the carriage that would take them there. Her trunks had been sent on ahead. Her mother refused to come but Jimmy had insisted. All of them had tears running down their cheeks as she boarded the train. It was the most difficult thing she had ever done. Jimmy, cried the loudest. She sensed that this could be forever and joined the travellers with a heavy heart.

After the train and carriage trip to the dock, she joined the passengers boarding the ship, "Lake Manitoba." The place was crowded with people, baggage, hawkers and odors, some she recognized and some she didn't. Managing to navigate through the people, she finally walked up the ramp to the ship and onto the deck, where she stood waving goodbye with tears running down her cheeks, saying quietly, "James, here I come, goodbye England, my dear family and home."

When she finally found her room, she sat down emotionally drained and weary. Soon, another girl about her age popped her head in and said, "Hello, I'm Margaret. Are you sailing alone?" Louise studied her face, and smiled.

"Yes, I am sailing alone. Going to meet my love, in Canada. I thought I would have a decent sized room."

"I know, but didn't you notice all the people getting on. This ship will be packed like sardines. I'm in the next compartment, so we can sit together."

It was the start of a good friendship. She was such a friendly jolly person. Something Louise needed desperately. Her reddish hair and pale complexion was in contrast to Louise and Margaret's blue eyes seemed to twinkle when she laughed. Louise found it difficult to relax and realized that she must focus on something other than what she left behind.

The two women talked at length. Louise told Margaret about her mother and all the difficulty she had. If it hadn't been for her father, she probably would never have left because she lacked the courage to argue with her mother.

After resting and sensing the ship was moving, they decided to look around. They wandered around the ship, just to get out and move. After a day at sea both girls got seasick. Most people on board were looking pale and listless. Fruit was passed around the deck and both girls tried to eat some but their appetites were not good. It took three or four days before people started to get some life back. No one was smiling, but at least they were starting to eat and move around. The food was palatable most of the time. Soon the girls got into a routine and spent most of their time on deck watching the endless waves and the birds flying behind. There was always a cool breeze so both women continued to wear their coats and hats. To them the water seemed to go on forever as they scoured the skyline for land. The two women stuck together sometimes having to distance themselves from displays of frustration and anguish. No one was prepared for the crowds on the ship which triggered fights. Some children were unruly and caused problems, often bringing the ship's crew running. They often mentioned how glad they would be to get to their destination.

Louise and Margaret would be parting ways when they landed at Halifax after ten days at sea. Louise was to take a train to Winnipeg to meet up with the Minister and his wife and the rest of the journey by Red River Cart train. What that was, she had no idea. As they disembarked, people were rushing and pushing, desperately trying to keep together. Parents were busy trying to hang on to their bags and their children. Louise tugged at her bag which wasn't heavy but it kept getting caught up in the luggage of other people. Margaret, bless her, was beside her as they disembarked and cried out when it was announced that there would be no supplies or arrangements made for the trip to Western Canada. She complained to Louise, "That bigshot, Rev. Barr, I think is a rat. He hasn't made any plans for us, and now, I hear he wants us to pay for his carriage to tour Halifax. The nerve!" Louise didn't know what to think about it but was sorry to say goodbye to Margaret who had been such an inspiration and fun, something she needed.

Louise was bewildered, she hadn't been too concerned about further travel. Her plans were already made. She waved goodbye again, and hurried to find out where to go to get the train to Winnipeg. After several attempts to ask the porters, she found one that understood her and directed her to a carriage that would take her to the station.

Chapter Two

Winnipeg

Finally, tired and hungry, Louise arrived in Winnipeg. As she stepped off the train, someone caught her by the arm, introducing himself as Rev. Walker and helped her with her bag. Taking her aside he presented his wife, Jean. It was coming back to her, the name, Walker. They escorted her to a waiting carriage and as she climbed in she wondered how they knew her. She would have to ask them or perhaps they had been told what she looked like.

"I have so much to tell you, Louise. The west is very uncivilized yet and there are so many obstacles for you to overcome," Jean said.

"I have no idea what to expect. James hasn't given me much information and what I gleaned from other people is not very reassuring," she stated.

In spite of everything, she liked these people. They were very welcoming and seemed to know a lot about her. Maybe she could ask them questions about what was troubling her.

The minister himself, was tall and slim with a ruddy but friendly face. His hair was a little long, she thought and his shoes were in need of repair. His wife was petite, with striking brown eyes that seemed to be always smiling. She also had long hair. They both made her feel comfortable so she thought maybe this was a good stop after all.

They talked at length over tea, and then Jean insisted that Louise rest for a while. They would wake her up for dinner and talk some more about her journey. After her rest and a good wash, she felt better and looked forward to further talks.

The reverend explained the Red River Cart wheels were all wood and leather so that as the cart proceeded, it made an ungodly screech and the oxen that pulled it were large. He talked at length about the cart train and the stops it made along the way. The carts could carry up to a thousand pounds. As he talked Louise just pushed the information to the back of her mind. She did get interested though when Jean mentioned the hard yeast cakes and some other techniques used out west. She mentioned the flies that bite. They gave her ointment that would help keep the flies away and some cream for the itch. Louise felt overwhelmed with all this information of oxen, flies, carts.

Soon she was about to leave the Walkers and thanked them wholeheartedly. Jean had given her a few things to put in her bag, just in case, she told her and the reverend added some netting. They told her so many things that she didn't know if she could remember it all.

The Trek West

Packed and ready to go, the Walkers took Louise to the station to embark on her last journey to Western Canada or the Northwest Territories as they called it, and James. She wasn't sure about anything at the moment. As she walked to the platform, she suddenly saw the oxen and stood frozen, startled at their size. A loud voice, brought her out of her shock and told her to climb aboard the cart. She lifted her coat just enough so she could reach the step up. The awful odors that assailed her nostrils were terrible but she was determined not to let it bother her. *It can't be any worse than around the factory.* She was to sit up on the front seat beside the drover who put her at ease, saying,

"Good morning, ma am - we need to get moving. We have a long way to go, so get comfortable and we will be off with the rest of the train."

Louise looked behind and noted more carts and covered wagons and some horseback riders forming quite a long train.

"I have never been on a cart before," she exclaimed.

The drover didn't answer right away. He was busy getting the oxen to move and watching all the other wagons. When he had time to answer, he had to shout to be heard above the noise," Then this will be a trip you will never forget. My name is Mike."

She acknowledged him, staring at his unruly beard and bushy eyebrows. She noted that his eyes were piercing but kind. Looking behind her, she noted that one trunk was in the cart. *Thank goodness, at least she would have a change of clothes.* As the wagons squeaked and squelched along she fought hard to keep her eyes open. They seemed to be following a path because she could see water, maybe a river. The weather was cool, so she was glad of her coat and tam. She found it hopeless to keep awake, in spite of the jolting and noise and soon was fast asleep, with her head resting on the drover's shoulder.

Around noon the train came to a stop and Louise woke up with a start. Mike advised her they would be passing out tea and biscuits and they would be resting the animals giving them food and water.

"Do I get down from the cart or wagon?" she asked.

"Not right now, relax. They will bring it to you."

Her back was aching already and this was just the start. Soon one of the men, who was clean shaven, a rare appearance by all she had seen, came by to check on her and offer her a cup of tea in a tin cup and a biscuit. It was certainly welcome and she thanked the fellow profusely. He nodded and smiled at her. She had noticed that all the other men seem to be bearded and scruffy. *I shouldn't judge a book by its cover.*

It wasn't long before the train began again. That same squeaking sound that seemed to echo for miles, hurt her ear drums, so she pulled her tam down over them. The weather was cool and felt like rain. The endless trees were leafy and green and she noted the odd rabbit dive into the brush. The cart lurched its way forward and soon the sun was setting low in a sky full of fluffy white clouds. She felt like she was in another world. Soon, they stopped and a hustle and bustle began. Fully awake, she watched the whole procedure with interest. The huge animals were set free of the wagon and taken away. She was mesmerized by the activity. Not knowing what to do, she just sat there looking around. She began to get nervous and started looking for somewhere to relieve herself. Before long another young woman came along and called her to come down and join her. That she did with difficulty, taking her time, so her dress wasn't torn and her coat soiled. She was glad of the company and delighted to see someone her own age. They were soon acquainted. Her name was Mary. She was a small person with dark brown eyes that seemed to twinkle. She filled her in as on what to expect and together they explored the brush around them. Mary seemed well aware of what was going on making Louise feel better.

They would be staying there for the night, she advised and that's when Louise saw what looked like just a shed, but when they went inside, it was furnished with bare bunks, a wooden table with benches and a wash stand.

"Is that all, we have to sleep on?"

"Yes, unless you want to sleep in the cart. There will be four of us women and we must stick together. Someone will be bringing us supper soon. I could smell something cooking," Mary shrugged matter of fact.

Finally, the other women joined them, weary and wanting to lay down, but waited patiently for their supper. Mary suggested they sit at the wooden table near the entrance after they had a chance to wash. Everything was rough, so Louise was careful with her dress and stockings.

The first one introduced was Margaret, a heavy set, stern looking woman, with very long graying hair and Nellie, who was tall and lanky, with a soft voice, and lovely curly brown hair. Mary was the smallest of them.

Mary invited them to use the outhouse, and told them that a pitcher of water would be brought for washing, adding, "You must all be tired and hungry, I know I am,"

At that moment, Mike, the drover, came in and spoke.

"Okay ladies, after supper, I would recommend that you get some rest. We will be leaving very early in the morning, right after you have had something to eat. We have a long way to go," and with that he turned, smiled at Louise, and strode out leaving a pile of blankets behind.

Louise studied Mike with renewed interest. There seemed to be so much hair, it was hard to distinguish his face. He wore a long skin coat like the other drovers and the smell of those coats was hard to avoid.

"Where do the men sleep. Are we using their quarters?" Louise asked,

"Oh, they have made their own arrangements, so don't worry," Mary stated.

When Louise looked outside, she realized that it was very dark. There was no way she could take a walk so she decided to get herself ready for bed and carefully unfolded the blankets, laying one underneath, covering herself with the another one and her coat. She was just dozing off when she heard the howl. It made her hair stand on end. She sat up at the same time as the other women.

"Coyotes, ladies, just talking to one another. They won't bother you. Go back to sleep," was Mary's quiet comment. *How did this girl know so much?* The howling continued but it didn't bother Louise, because she had stuck hankies in her ears. It dulled the noise and this she would do much of the trek especially the noise of the carts which was almost unbearable. *Worse than the streets of Leeds.*

Morning dawned early, and Louise marveled at the beads of dew on the grass that looked like little diamonds and the fresh air which was so welcome when she went to the outhouse. Her stomach was aching, not from hunger but from the jostling of the cart. She longed to be home at this point. Tea would be welcome but she had no appetite at all and groaned when she thought about lunch or dinner. As usual tea and biscuits, jam and cheese, was dispersed.

Soon the drovers indicated they were anxious to get moving. "You never know when we have a hold up or problems along the way," Mike told Louise, while she tackled getting up into the wagon. She didn't want to know what lay ahead, so she kept quiet.

Thus, the journey started slowly at first, then picked up a little speed at the urgency of the drovers. They squeaked their way along, but Louise had become smart and again stuffed a hankie in each ear, pulling her tam down over top. She looked funny, she knew, but it helped more than anything. The other women had adopted a similar method. As they bumped ahead, it lulled Louise to sleep again, only this time she was dreaming of home and awoke with a start when they stopped for the noon break and lunch. She waited until her tea and biscuits came, then climbed down for a stretch. The procedure was becoming routine. It was company she needed not rest so she went in search of Mary and the other women whom she had heard singing hymns.

Nellie, the tall, thin one wanted to be alone and disappeared, but Louise and Margaret decided they had best go in search of her. Just as they saw her, so did Mike. He nodded to the women putting his hand to his mouth to be quiet. They couldn't imagine why, but followed orders. He carried a whip that he let loose with a grand snap, scaring them both. Nellie, was sitting on a flat stone on the bank of a creek, where the sun shone through the trees. What Nellie didn't see was something sunning itself on the next stone. The drover was a good shot and knocked the snake off the stone and into the water. Nellie turned frightened at the noise and seeing the snake flying through the air, screamed and fainted. Louise and Margaret rushed to her side, but Mike was quicker and picked her up and carried her back to the train. He set her on a blanket and went for some water, asking the women to stay with her. She finally came to and smiled weakly at the women.

"I guess I won't be doing that again." By the time they were ready to leave, she was back to her old self. Mary came to explain that to wander off could be folly,

"So, please don't do it, ladies," she added emphatically. It gave them food for thought during the next few hours on board the wagon. Louise wondered again about Mary and why she was on this trek but still hadn't asked her.

After they got going again, Louise thought maybe there was something bothering Nellie. Perhaps we can help her! Louise mulled it all over in her mind while the wagon squeaked on. She watched the poor oxen for a while, then as her mind turned back to Nellie, she remembered what the Rev. Walker had told her 'don't forget to pray.' I will talk to Margaret tonight before we retire, we should pray with Nellie. She may need a friend. At that thought she smiled and watched as the trees swished by the wagon.

Never had she seen so many trees, shrubs, some flowering trees, some so thick, no one could get through. Sometimes there would be a break in the landscape and then you could see for miles. She tried to identify some of the shrubs, but found it daunting. When the wagons finally stopped, the sky was ablaze with a million stars. She stared at them, mesmerized. As she climbed down, she whispered, "I'll be there soon, James, "wondering if he was looking at the stars too as she went to find the other women.

The women sat together while they ate their evening meal of beef stew inside the shed or bunk house as they started to call it. Margaret was talkative but Nellie was still despondent. Finally, as they finished, Louise asked Nellie if she could pray for her. Nellie started to cry.

"It'll be okay, Nellie, talk to us?"

She started slowly, crying periodically as she explained how she had married quite young and that her husband had decided to immigrate, to follow that old minister that came to their church bragging up this country and its grand opportunities. Her husband couldn't be persuaded not to go, so she helped him with money and hadn't heard from him since he left a year ago.

"I don't know what I will find, or even if he is in Saskatoon, anymore," she agonized.

Louise interrupted and said, "lets say a prayer for her," and they did. Nellie stopped crying and nodded to the women as she dabbed at her nose and dried her tears.

"God will help us," Margaret suddenly spoke. "My husband is also one of those men, that listened to that Rev. Barr. He thought it sounded so wonderful. He borrowed money from his father to go and promised faithfully that he would send for me. He didn't, but I will find him. I never received a letter so I decided to come and look for myself. How bad can it be?" she finished and after that statement, the women vowed to help each other and climbed into bed, but before they did, all of them covered their ears. It was the beginning of a friendship that would sustain them. They learned to use the netting to cover themselves at night. With the warmth came the flies.

Chapter Three

The next day and the next was the same, but on the following day, they ran into some problems. It had rained in the night and the path was awash in places and muddy in others, so much so that the women were asked to get off the wagons and walk beside to help the animals. There was water everywhere. The women, anxious not to get their shoes and dresses wet, looked around for what to do, when Mary showed up and suggested they take off their shoes and stockings, and draw their dresses up at the waist. Mary, had changed into pants and rubber boots. Louise wished they had some boots, too. They had long ago put their coats in the back of the wagon. Louise followed orders with Mike watching, making her blush. They did not ask them to push, but when Louise saw what was happening, she decided to help, as did the other women. The mud was thick, sucking their feet in with every step. Slowly they moved, so slowly, slipping and sliding at times, feeling like they were hardly moving. It was hard on their tender feet. They encountered sticks and stones and the drovers hollered to watch for dung. When Louise came across it, she felt like gagging. It was a herculean effort for all of them to keep the oxen moving and the wagons with their loads although some had been removed to be lifted over later. The oxen looked weary as well for they moved slowly, straining with every step, their tails swatting at the flies that followed them in hordes. The men were shouting and prodding, while pushing as well.

Most of the day was spent by the time they all got to higher ground. The women were played out and muddy, but were allowed to climb aboard. Louise couldn't wait to wash her feet and the hem of her dress was worse than she thought. It had come loose in numerous places and dragged in the mud. What a mess they were in.

Finally, they could hear the welcome sound of gurgling water. The stream was a happy sight. The oxen must have heard it too, for they had started moving more quickly. When they finally stopped, the women climbed down and rushed to the water, but Mary was there advising them to wait and brought a pail to catch water. Beyond the path was a creek, running quite swiftly over some logs, an ideal spot to wash, but they were advised to wash in the basin at the bunk house. The women looked at one another and started to laugh, while continuing to swat flies away.

"Who shall go first?" said Margaret. Louise nodded and followed her to the bunk house saying, "You can," as they noted the sound of the men talking. Laughing and splashing, they cleaned themselves, attempting to wash the hems of their dresses as well. They periodically looked out at the swift running water, silently wishing they could have waded in. Afterwards the women sat outside on a log to let their dresses and feet dry.

They would again say a prayer for all of them. However, after drying off, the itch began just as they were sitting down to eat. They scratched as they ate, feeling bruises and scrapes as well that would need tending.

"My ankles, whatever did we get into?" Nellie cried. Mary, realizing they had been bitten by mosquitos spoke up, "Mosquitos, ladies, I do have some lotion and I have some ointment for your feet."

"Rev. Walker gave me some ointment and cream, he said I might need along the way. Is that what he was talking about?" answered Louise.

"I would say so," answered Mary. "You need to find it if you can,"

Louise, quickly put her stockings and shoes back on and trudged back to the wagon to get her bag. Going through it, she found the tins and took them back. She needed a change of bloomers too but did not have time to change.

The cream did help them and they were able to sleep that night, although they would have probably slept anyway after scratching until they were bloodied. Their feet were so tender. Most of the rest of their body was covered which they declared was a blessing.

Mary explained about the scarf that Louise had brought back, was to be made into a triangle to be tied at the back of the neck. Then they could bring the scarf up over their nose and mouth if necessary to protect them against the sun and wind and bugs or they could put it on their heads. She was worried about them getting sunburned. They all nodded, understanding her completely for their cheeks were already rough and sore.

Days ran into nights, until Louise felt she could not endure any more. The food was okay, but she was getting tired of beans and stews and the continual flies that hovered over everything. The flapjack cakes she liked. Her mouth watered thinking about them. They offered coffee, but she had never drank coffee, and although she did try she preferred tea.

Her body felt like it would never recover. She dreamed of taking a bath and walking about without someone watching all the time. She asked Mary about her trip and she told her the Ministers in Winnipeg had asked her to accompany the women. The men had been warned to stay away from them, under threat.

The days dragged on, each one the same. The landscape was still the same, trees, and big open spaces, streams, lots of water, strange animals, tremendous amount of bugs and the rough talk among the men, which of course, she was used to from the streets of Leeds. The days were warming up and the warmth and the constant jiggling often made her drowsy. The smelly concoction she had, kept the flies away from her and Mike.

As they drove, Mike, suddenly, turned to her and asked her to get into the back of the wagon and cover up. She looked at him bewildered until she heard the drums.

"The Indians may be on the war path. In any case they will try to steal all our food and provisions and maybe you women."

That statement motivated her and she moved quickly, tearing her dress in her haste climbing into the back of the wagon. She covered with her blanket, but kept enough of an opening so she could see what was going on. Her ankles were itchy, instead of her lotion she found her ointment and put some on her hand. Feeling eyes on her, she looked up, and froze momentarily. Staring at her beside the trunk was a painted face. He hollered, and it leashed something inside her. She screamed at him and lashed out with everything she had and hit him squarely across the mouth. He coughed and backed off, spitting and dancing around. He kept spitting making a funny noise. What she did not realize is that the hand that hit him had some of the smelly ointment on it. The men seeing what had happened and what she had done, were clapping and calling, "Bravo."

The wagons had stopped and everyone was edgy including the women who were in a state of shock. Mike hollered, "It's that smelly stuff you been using," and watched for any other riders lurking around. Then they saw the 'redcoats' as Louise called them, behind them and coming up fast. The leader, called to Mike as he rode up beside the wagons, hollering, "Watch for scouts, there may be more then one."

The one that Louise smacked was long gone on his horse but the train was now very uneasy. They stood watching and waiting for another one to appear. They could hear the redcoats checking the brush and moving ahead of them. They were told to start moving, so Mike gave the go ahead. Louise was still lying in the back. She never moved a muscle and even forgot about the itching. She did keep some ointment on her hand though, just in case. Her nerves were raw and she thought at one point she was going to faint. She stared at the redcoats, as they rode beside the wagon, smiling at her. It was reassuring to see them, but she groaned when she heard the drums again.

One of the "redcoats" came riding up to the wagon and told them that, the other two scouts had been found and were retreating.

"Just keep watch, remember we are ahead of you and will remain ahead. We don't want to lose the provisions that you have on board," as he saluted, smiled, turned and rode off.

Louise threw off her blanket and prepared to get up. She wanted to get back on the seat, so she could at least see what was going on. Mike, however, spoke up saying, "Stay put for a little while. We will be stopping soon."

"Goodness, is it that time already," she called

It had been one heck of a day so far. Her nerves were still pretty raw and the rest of the women would be the same, having never ever heard or seen Indians, except maybe in pictures. Night came and although they were nervous, they were tired and slept with no problems. When they started moving again in the morning, she noted there was no sign of the redcoats and it made her worry. She would have to ask Mike about that.

As soon as they started in a steady gait, she ventured to ask Mike,

"I haven't seen any of the redcoats. They said they would be ahead of us."

"Yeah, they did, and I suspect they are, but quite a way ahead. They know and understand the Indians and usually they negotiate with them, help them. I don't think they really want to hurt anyone. By the way, the one you clobbered, had probably never seen a white woman before, that's why he was looking at you. He may have seen you sitting up front, because they usually follow for quite a way, checking on the load. He was enamored with you and couldn't help but try to get a closer look. I will never forget, the look on his face, after you hit him."

"Even with all that paint on his face?" she added.

"Yes, even with all that so-called war paint. That was the best fun we have had in months. The boys, really think you are something," he said laughing heartedly

"They what?"

"You have made a name for yourself on this journey."

Louise sat back and couldn't believe what she was hearing. No wonder, during the meal last night and tea this morning, the men were all smiling and nodding to her. Normally, they didn't pay much attention. They were always in a hurry to feed them and ask if there is anything they can do to make them comfortable. Oh well, today is another day and with that she leaned back and relaxed, trying to enjoy the scenery such as it was. She had dozed off, when Mike announced the midday break, and immediately got busy watering and feeding the big beasts.

After the break, the day cooled off, but the wagons started moving. Dark clouds appeared in the horizon and Louise commented to Mike on it.

"Yeah," replied Mike "storm coming, I would say. We'll try to make it to our next stop. Have you ever seen or heard of a thunder storm yet?" he asked. Louise shook her head.

"The weather in England could be rough at times, we got lots of rain," she answered.

"You are in for a treat then, be prepared," and with that he turned his attention to the oxen.

They moved along smoothly, while the wheels screeched, but Louise was now well prepared for that. Soon, she was dozing off and dreaming of meeting up with James. She couldn't wait! A clap of thunder, brought her out of her slumber. In an instant she was wide awake and looking about.

"We are about to stop. I want you to go quickly to the shelter, before the rain starts, and put your coat back on."

Soon the whole team had stopped and drovers were looking after the bawling animals. The women gathered and made for the shelter, which was a simple framework of poles. One of the poles in the roof was missing, so they wondered about keeping dry if it rained when Mary came running with a skin. "Quickly ladies, the storm is coming up fast. Let's get under cover. This skin will go over our heads to keep us dry." As she explained this, the thunder clapped again but before it did, Louise watched the entire sky light up and let out a cry. Nellie and Margaret were fascinated as well. None of them had ever seen such a display. The thunder clapped and lightning flashed coming one after the other. They watched in silence as the storm came closer. Suddenly the wind picked up, and the trees started swaying back and forth. They had to hang on to the skin, each holding one side. Underneath, they sat wrapped in a blanket sitting on a bunk. There was no way they were going to sleep in this storm. As the storm progressed, the rain started and came through the hole in the so-called roof, but they managed to keep dry.

Nellie's expression was, "God is raining buckets on us," and they all agreed. Margaret decided she would pray, whether the rest did or not. They all joined in, closing their eyes to the devastation outside. They could hear the men calling and the animals bawling, but they couldn't see anything. As it rained, Louise wondered if everyone had shelter.

When night fell, the storm eased, the lightning and thunder quit and the rain turned to a mist. Only then did the woman finally get some sleep, even though the air was damp and cool, but they were free of mosquitos for the time being.

Morning dawned bright and sunny. Louise marveled at the blue sky. They were all hungry having no supper the night before, but as they arose from their sleep, Mary, bless her, came with tea and those flapjacks, but they were different. They were rolled up around a sausage and dipped in sugar. Louise couldn't wait to get one and oh how she needed a cup of tea.

"Mary, you are a life saver. However, did you get this?"

"Oh, cook, saw the storm coming and prepared these ahead of time, knowing full well that we would not be getting any supper. He was up very early, getting the stove started and brewing tea. He is a wonder, that man."

That day the wagons moved at a good clip, and the men were more jovial. Mike, explained to Louise that she was nearing the end of her journey. "You will be glad of that, I am sure. It has been a long hard time," he said. Louise asked to talk to the cook.

"Why?" he asked.

"I like those what did he call them, flap cakes?" she answered.

"Oh, you mean flapjacks or pancakes. Sure, we will be stopping for a break soon, you can ask him then. He will be pleased that someone liked them. He's a bit gruff, but talk to him," nodding with a smile.

When they stopped for the noon break, Louise, quickly jumped down from the wagon. She was getting pretty good at getting up and down, as were the other women. She waited until people started moving around to go in search of the cook. She had seen him periodically, but didn't know his name. He was always clean shaven and had a round face, with a kerchief on his head. *Funny, his hair must be very short, and perhaps he had no hair.* She found him busy already starting a fire in the little stove. He looked up surprised saying, "Yeah, what can I do for you, ma am?" *He didn't sound so gruff.*

"I like those flap cakes you make, and I would like to know how to make them?" As he kept walking back and forth, moving bags, he stopped and looked at her as if seeing her for the first time. Quickly he regained his composure and answered, "I will give you the recipe when we arrive at our destination," smiling broadly. Louise blushed and looked away, quietly saying, "Thank you."

She must start planning and picking up hints instead of dreaming and wishing away time. This was all so new to her. She was beginning to look forward to the end of this trek.

Chapter Four

Destination Lashburn

After their rest, the wagon train resumed the trip. Everyone was quite jovial and Louise could hear the women singing. It really lifted her spirits and she started to sing with them. And sing they did, loud and long. Smiling, Louise, thought they would scare the rabbits right out of their holes and laughed out loud. Even Mike had to laugh at the sound and sight of Louise. They brought some kind of lightheartedness to the train and the beasts that drove it. As she watched those animals, she stared amazed how majestic they were, as they strained with their load day after day. She had come to recognize the value in these quiet, docile animals and marveled at the ability of the drovers and riders on the train. It will be something to tell my grandchildren, she thought, smiling.

It seemed the animals were moving along faster as the day went on. Mike informed her that they should make their destination within a day or so. That night, she stuffed her hankie in her ears, and drifted off dreaming of James and of home, first feeling elated and then feeling sad. She drifted in and out of those feelings, leaving her fretful in the morning, even though the mood was jovial.

Louise had no idea of what to expect when they arrived. She promised herself to keep an open mind and tried to remember what the Rev. Walker had told her. She wished she had paid more attention to everything he told her and had taken notes. She blamed herself for missing so much and felt she would have to learn the hard way.

Louise had only one thought that prevailed throughout and that was that she would soon see her beloved James again. Louise always enjoyed looking at the twinkling stars at night and thinking James would be looking at those same stars. 'Soon, James, soon,' she said to herself every time as she drifted off to sleep, hoping against hope that this would be the last night.

The next day dawned bright and sunny. There was blue sky as far as the eye could see. However, she noticed the lack of trees, something she hadn't noticed before. She mentioned that and how weary they were to the others while they drank their tea. Margaret sighed and folded her hands to pray and the others joined in. They learned to ignore the ruddy cheeked, whiskered men looking at them smiling and watching. They had learned to trust the drovers.

Back in the wagons, they trudged on, watching the endless horizon for civilization. As the day dragged on, someone yelled, "We are almost there," and you could feel the excitement in the air. In the distance, they could barely see a smattering of shacks. There were only a couple of two story houses, along with what looked like sheds, but tears obliterated Louise' vision.

"Is that my destination?" she cried. Shock kept her from saying any more. She could not believe this was where James was. She watched as they drew closer, hoping and praying that this wasn't her destination.

As they got closer, she could hear women and men coming towards them, arms waving and calling out a welcome. She looked at Mike for some explanation, but he was waving back and laughing and calling to them. As they pulled up in front of a two story clapboard house, Mike indicated to Louise this was her stop. Stunned she looked at him but followed his instructions. This just could not be!

Getting down, she stumbled towards the house, collapsing on the front steps, still thinking it was wrong. She started to cry, but through her sobs, she heard her name being called, "Louie, Louie, it's me."

"Oh, James, is that you?" she sobbed. That was a voice she hadn't heard for a long time but there was a stranger coming towards her, and she was afraid. He had long hair and beard, and his clothes were ragged and dusty. She sneezed as she peered closer. Suddenly, she realized it was James. Looking up at him through her tears, she nodded and still sobbing lifted her arms to him and they clung together for a long time, until he moved to help her up. Only then did he speak again in a teary voice.

"Louie, I am so thankful you have come. I need you so, but first, I know how tired you must be and have arranged for you to stay here, until we can make other arrangements. Mrs. Long, will look after you." As he was talking, Mrs. Long came out the door and motioned to them. "Please, come in and set yourself down.

You can meet some of the other women that have journeyed here and rest yourself after you have had some tea."

Before Louise moved, the cook was at her side and handed her a piece of paper saying, "I promised you this, Ma'am," and quickly turned back to his covered wagon.

James, looked at Louise, in askance. Only then did Louise brighten up and smile saying she would explain later. James hesitated momentarily before patting her on the back saying, "Rest, tonight, my love, and I will see you tomorrow."

After her tea, she was escorted to a bedroom. It contained a bed, something she hadn't seen since Winnipeg, a washstand and a chair. Mrs. Long brought her a pitcher of warm water, soap and a towel and told her where the outhouse was. After a wash, she collapsed on the bed and awoke to the sun streaming through the window and the tantalizing aroma of food cooking. She got up quickly, still feeling stiff and sore, but at least the thought of not having to get into that wagon again gave her a lift. After she washed again, she wandered downstairs to the dining/sitting room, and was greeted by Mrs. Long. She really hadn't noticed the lady, the day before. She had a long face, suiting her name, thought Louise, but it was a friendly face. She wore a long white apron over her dress and her hair was tied back nicely but Louise thought her shoes could use some help. Although they had just met she felt like an old friend.

"You have slept for over 12 hours, Louise. That must have felt good after your trek?" she asked.

"You have no idea," she answered. "Has my trunk arrived?"

"Yes, it has and it is over there by the door."

"I need some fresh clothes desperately." She said as she tested the trunk and found it to be very heavy.

"Oh, no, this is the wrong trunk. This one has my sewing machine, and other supplies in it. What am I going to do? I have no other clothes," she cried, hanging her head and shrugging her shoulders.

"First of all my name is Liz, and like all of us, Louise, you will make out fine. I'll give you a dress for now, until your other trunk arrives. We'll make do! Give me your clothes and I can wash them for you. The wind has picked up so they will dry quickly."

Louise sighed murmuring, "Thank you so much," looking at her and noting that they were about the same height and weight. Curiosity got the better of her then and she asked,

"By the way Mrs. Long/Liz, however did you get to this place?"

"My husband and I immigrated from Holland, some years ago. We were young and my husband was a baker, and I had some baking experience, so we decided to find a place to start a business. When we got to Edmonton, we procured a team and wagon and thought to go west and only got this far when a wheel came off. It was a disaster, and we ended up at this house, run by an English man and his wife. They desperately wanted to go back home, so we made an agreement to take over and pay them when we could. It all started out fine. I don't know why I am telling you all this," she hesitated. When Louise smiled and asked her to continue. "My husband got the flu and by the time a doctor got here, he was gone. I didn't know what to do, but people were so kind to me, coming in every day, that I just continued on and little by little it grew and here I am. Sorry but I must get back to work. Soon we will be joined by two other ladies, that have come across the water like you," as tears spilled down her face.

"Thank you for telling me and yes, I would like to meet them," Louise answered. *I will feel a lot better if there were more women here.*

"Sit down and have some tea, Louise. The other ladies will be here shortly," said Liz When the tea came, she sipped it, carefully not to spill a drop. Savoring the time of peace and quiet and the soft chair she sat in. I will never under estimate a chair ever again, and how did the drover know where to stop? she muttered, not realizing that she could be heard. And indeed Mrs. Long or Liz, did hear and answered her question.

"Well. those drovers have been across the West many times, and know this country like the back of their hand, besides, I would imagine they were given specific instructions. I am well known along this line and often have visitors that come with them. I can't imagine sitting on one of those wagon seats for any length of time, my dear, I can assure you."

"One doesn't realize how important such small things are until you don't have them," Louise answered.

"By the way does this place have a name? Also what happened to the other women that came with me"

"Oh, not really, this is part of the British colony that was engineered by Rev. Barr. Those women you are asking about continued on to Saskatoon by carriage, I was told."

Suddenly the door burst open and two women came hurrying in. Mrs. Long was at the door in an instant to welcome them. She introduced the women to Louise, Miss Taylor and Mrs. Ward. To which Miss. Taylor responded, "call me Amelia." and Mrs. Ward said, "call me Meg." Both women had pleasant faces, Amelia (Amy) was short and maybe a bit over weight, with lips weighted down with lipstick, and cheeks heavily rouged, and Meg was tall and thin, with a very pleasant smile that created a dimple in her cheek. Amy had light brown curly hair while Meg had very long dark hair pulled back severely in a bun. Both wore a small hat and long dresses which Louise thought could be English.

"Are you from England? Did you by any chance come on the ship called, 'The Manitoba?'" she asked. When both ladies responded with a strong, "Yes!" Laughter erupted.

"I have never been so pushed and shoved in all my life," uttered Amy.

"Disrespectful, I tell you," cried Meg.

The discussion about the ship went on for some time. Louise finally turned the conversation over to the present, asking where they were headed. Amy spoke up and declared that she thought her fiancé to be was somewhere near Saskatoon, and when she inquired, was directed to this place. I haven't seen him or heard from him in a while, but he did want me, I know."

Meg was reluctant to say much, but added, "I followed my heart, maybe I was wrong, but I couldn't wait any longer. After all, we made plans to always be together."

Louise wondered how they got to this place, the way they were dressed. She would have to ask them. Obviously, they had not come on the Wagon Train.

Mrs. Long was listening to all the conversation, but did not say a word. She was studying Louise when she came up with an idea. Something Louise said gave her a clue.

"Louise, how would you like to bake some bread for me tomorrow and perhaps you could show these ladies what to do?" Before she even finished her question, Louise answered.

"Oh, yes, that I would like. It would make me feel more comfortable living here. I don't have any yeast though," she uttered.

"I have yeast cakes, and you can set them to soak overnight, if you wish?"

"How about it ladies, your first lesson or do you know what to do?"

"I have never baked in my life," said Amy.

"I have done some cooking, but not bread," replied Meg.

At that moment, the door burst open and two men entered. "James," called Louise, rushing to hug him, with his long scraggly hair and beard.

"John, is that you?" cried Amy, not moving from her chair. John was stunned. He hadn't heard a word from her and here she was. He stood frozen to the spot until James nudged him.

" You talked about her long enough, man, go to her," James urged him.

John rushed across the room and picked Amy up and swung her around, like she was a little girl. He couldn't stop smiling. Then he stopped, looking at James. "What are we going to do?" looking around wildly, adding, "I have no place to take her."

James answered him saying, "We will think this out."

James looked at Louise lovingly and asked, "Did you by any chance bring your hair cutting supplies?"

"It happens to be the trunk that came with me," she sighed. "And yes, I can't wait to cut both your hair and beard right after you have your tea." She knew the way they looked at the table how hungry they were.

Mrs. Long came to the rescue calling from the kitchen, "bacon and eggs, coming up."

Louise rose and went to the kitchen to help, while the other women, said they would gladly wash up while the hair cutting took place.

The men wolfed down the meal as she watched. *I came just in time.* When they sat back with their tea, James looked at her with such love, she thought she would melt.

Refusing to leave John, Amy was reluctant to help Meg in the kitchen. Meg, however insisted and Amy finally gave in collecting dishes as she went. Louise immediately left to get her cutting shears and found a cape to put around the neck as well.

Motioning for James to come, she ushered him outside, where he grabbed her and hugged her. She managed to keep her scissors out of harms way. She hugged him back, but was determined to get to work on his hair and so pushed him onto a chair just outside the door where there was a small landing before the stairs. His hair was a tangled mess. She spent the next few minutes trying to comb it but gave up and started cutting. It took some work but she was determined to do it. After an hour, she had accomplished a great deal with his hair and started on his beard which was wiry and tough. While she worked, he talked to her about his partners, John Wily, who was with him and Bill who was not well. Finally, she gave him the go ahead to find a mirror and look. Then she called for John to come and take his place.

When John saw James, he whistled, and that brought everyone out to see. There were exclamations all around. John seated himself and Louise drew the cloth around his neck in a hurry. She worked on his hair and beard for another hour and Amy was the first to holler and clap when she saw him. They were laughing and crying all at the same time.

It was such a small thing but for the men it was immense, thought Louise. She silently thanked her father for making sure she had her scissors. How did he know? She was also glad that she had some experience in cutting hair. She grew quiet, when she thought of young James, and his reddish hair and all the times she spent with him not only cutting his hair but playing with him. Jolted by the talk around the table, she sighed and smiled.

By the time everyone settled down, James nodded to John, "We must get going or it will be dark and it will cost us another day."

"Sorry, Amy, we must go, but we will be back soon." As he looked at her fondly, she started to cry,

"I want to go with you," she exclaimed, hanging on to him.

"No, my darling, there is no where for you to stay just yet. We are working on a solution, I promise. Now no more tears, I am sure the ladies here will give you some necessary information about the wild west," he said as he kissed her brow. At that point, she shook her head and let go of his arm.

Louise spoke up then. "Amy, you and I will be going as soon as is possible. I have faith in James and John. And we will pray for them," she added, setting the stage for religion. Pleased, James doffed his cap to the women and took off in a hurry. They still had to load their wagon with goods before going home. He had told them he was concerned about Bill, whom they had left with enough supplies for a day, but you never know what might happen while away.

Hurrying out the door after them, Louise called to James. " I have some soup for your friend, drop back and I will have it ready." She hoped he had heard her. She ran to her trunk and fished out the desiccated soups and went to the kitchen, to ask Liz for a pot so she could make it up and ask how she was going to transport it after she made it. Liz was quite ready for the question and suggested she prepare the soup and she would give her a glass jar with a lid to put it in and a towel to wrap it. She added, "It won't stay warm, but they can warm it up for him when they get home. He probably will need it by then."

"What a blessing you are, Liz. Whatever, could we do without you?" at which all the women nodded.

They were all a bit tired, and showed it, yawning and looking weary all of a sudden. Amy, of course, was still feeling a little down, but maintained a quiet stance. Now with the men gone, they all retired to their rooms except Louise. She went digging through her trunk to see what her mother might have stuck in her trunk besides the soups. When she did not find anything else, she also laid down for just a nap but fell fast asleep, waking in the dead of night to the howling of the coyotes. Something she thought she would never get used to. Tomorrow, she promised herself, she would take a look outside at this treeless, barren land.

The next day turned out to be, calm, warm and very quiet. Louise woke up, excited and ready to tackle her bread making lessons. She was a little concerned about Amy, because she did not seem to care about cooking or learning for that matter. Pursing her lips, she muttered, " I will try and instill some habits in her for her own sake," as she made her way to the kitchen.

The kitchen was empty, she noted, looking around for the other two girls she was to teach. Oh well, she would begin. Gathering up the supplies she needed and the soaked yeast cake, she began. She was wondering about the girls when the door opened and in they came. They had been outside to look around and realized that they were late for their lesson.

"Sorry, Louise, I wanted to look around outside and I didn't realize the time," Meg nodded toward the door.

"It was my fault," said Amy. We got carried away looking in the General Store."

"A General Store? Now girls, the bread awaits you, let's go. Wash your hands, please," she asked quietly, not wanting to sound too demanding.

"Right," both spoke at once and raced to the basin of water.

Louise began by telling them the items in the recipe and the amounts to be used. She brought out the large bowl that Liz told her to use and proceeded to explain the procedure. As they worked, she noted that Meg got right into the process without hesitation, but Amy never took part. She wanted the two to knead the dough but only Meg did, until it was time to place it in the bowl to rise. Then she asked them if they would like some tea and proceeded to make it. Of course, they were both eager to sit.

"Amy, if you are going to be of any use to John, you must make some effort to do these things," Louise spoke sternly.

"I don't think I can do that," she answered.

"Why ever not?" asked Meg.

"I would rather hire someone to do it, like Louise," and before Louise could answer that, she added, "my dad gave me money for such things."

Louise and Meg looked at each other in surprise. "Have you ever cooked or cleaned, Amy?" asked Meg.

"Well-l, not really. We had a cook, and a maid and a gardener to do the menial tasks."

This was a revelation. Meg was first to answer her, " Amy, there is no one here to hire, and if you are thinking of Louise, she has her own man to look after miles away. It is not possible." At that point Amy began to cry.

"Crying isn't going to solve anything, Amy. You either have to buck up and learn some things or you will not last. You know it is called the wild west for a reason. There is no sitting on your fanny here. And what about John? Doesn't he deserve to have help? If you love that man, you must do everything in your power to make this work," Louise finished the last few words emphatically.

"No one can sit around here doing nothing. You would be bored to tears. Did you not read the pamphlets we were given?" said Meg shaking her head wildly.

"I guess I didn't think it applied to me. Daddy said I could have all the money I wanted within reason. We have always had servants."

"Come girls the bread is ready for the pans. Amy, you are going to do this. Now watch me, and then try it," called Louise.

Amy watched closely and then tried it. She made a loaf, sort of. Louise nodded. It would have to do. Louise kept wondering if they couldn't turn this girls thinking around for John's sake she will end up going home and he would be devastated. *I should talk to Liz and Meg about it and maybe between us all, we can help.*

The rest of the day went quietly, but the women asked Amy to talk to them. There were questions they needed to ask her. "What did you bring with you and what did you expect?" However, Amy wasn't prepared to give any information yet.

Towards the end of the day, a couple of men came into the home asking about a hair cutter. When Louise spoke up, they both wanted to pay her to cut their hair. But Louise has other ideas. "Come in. If you buy a lunch here from Mrs. Long, I will cut your hair for free," leaving the other women with their mouths open, except Liz, who was elated.

"No problem, lady," they answered in unison sitting themselves down at a table.

Word got around and soon, Louise was inundated with requests to cut hair. Meg pitched in to do some of the cooking for Liz and Amy, well, she was not contributing anything but complaints. Louise continued to make bread for Liz and oh, did Liz appreciate that. She was getting a much needed rest, since she was the only one in the place that was a cafe come boarding rooms. It wasn't a large menu, just everyday good food.

Amy, of course, always wanted special service. Meg and Louise worried about John, who was about to set a claim on the land next to James and order what he needed for a house or Soddy as they called it. He was excited to get going on his own and with the help of neighbors and James and Bill, he would make it. However, he had to have help from the female portion of the family too. Louise had an idea. When her other trunk came, and James came in, she would ask him if her and Amy could make the trip out to their home. She did not have any idea what it was like either, so it would serve two purposes. She thought about this at length and posed the idea to Meg and Liz. Both agreed it wouldn't hurt and maybe it would give Amy a nudge to start doing some of the menial things around Liz's business.

When Amy finally came out of her bedroom, disheveled and grumpy, Louise asked her about her idea and within minutes, she completely changed and clapped her hands and twirled around the cafe. "Mind you, Amy, you must keep an open mind, after all we are in new territory and everything is different," Louise admonished her, then added, " Prepare yourself, it will be a long hard ride in a wagon. However, we will take lunch along and I hope be able to stop somewhere nice to eat it. Also, it depends on the men, if they will go for it."

"I can't wait to see John, he will be so excited," Amy was still in a peppy mood and everyone was watching her, but with trepidation. They knew what kind of person she had shown them.

Sounds of people running and shouting forced all of them to run to the door to see what was going on, that is all except Liz. She already knew that a wagon train was just pulling into the place and people were excited to get some provisions and necessary items that they ordered.

Out on the street, dust and noise, prevented the three women from going out into the street as well. The excitement Louise could understand after being there herself. She hoped her trunk was on that train. She was having a hard time staying put, wanting to know about it. Suddenly one of the wagons stopped in front of the women and announced that a trunk would be delivered. Louise let out a whoop and clapped her hands in delight.

Later that afternoon, her trunk was delivered and she felt a great deal of relief to have more clothes to wear. She must wash the dress she was wearing and repair it before giving it back to Liz for being so generous. She was thinking about it when a couple wagon drovers came in asking for something to eat and could they please have a place to wash up. The women nodded and pointed and then retreated, for they were dusty and dirty and smelly. Liz ignored it all and was in the kitchen preparing a meal for the hungry men. Soon others would be coming, so she engaged the women to set tables and help in the kitchen. All nodded except Amy, she went back into her room and never came out until all the drovers had gone claiming, "I couldn't stand being next to those stinky men. Who are they anyway?" she asked pertly

"Amy, for heavens sakes, how do you think I got here, if it wasn't for those men. They are the hardest working individuals I have ever seen and perfect gentlemen." Louise was getting tired of Amy and her ways. She was beginning to regret having asked about taking her out to the farm. Goodness knows what she will want to do.

The women, all but Amy, cleaned up and put everything away and set the tables for morning. They were all a little tired and soon drifted off to their rooms.

Next morning looked beautiful, not a cloud in the sky. The air was sweet smelling, but Louise could not identify what made it smell so sweet. She noted the grasses were starting to yellow giving the whole area a golden look. It looked lovely! She wondered if James would be in town today. She was anxious to go out to the farm and find out for herself what it was like and she would make the best of it and maybe help bring Bill back to a better life. She made her own tea and sat down to drink it. Contented for the moment, she decided to make bread and help in the kitchen along with Meg, who had already finished her tea and started cooking. The day passed quickly. No one had seen or heard from Amy.

"Louise, do you think it is wise to take this girl out with you?" asked Meg.

"I have to try for John's sake," she answered, at which Meg nodded in agreement.

When Amy did show, all smartly dressed, with make up on and her hair all done up, indicating she had spent most of the day getting dressed and made up. They were stunned. Then when she added a fancy hat to the outfit and walked around smartly, it was as if she was turning her nose up at all of them.

"And where does she think she's going? To the opera?" called Liz from the kitchen.

Just then a wagon appeared outside the door and suddenly they heard Amy's high pitched voice calling, "John, oh, John."

Louise was also excited.

John jumped down from the wagon, but when Amy went to grab him, he pushed her away. "I am dusty and dirty, I need to wash up before I can hug you, Amy. Why are you dressed like that?" He didn't sound angry just surprised.

Louise ran out and motioned to them calling, "You must be hungry? Tie up the horses and come in and have something to eat and drink."

Amy just stood there for a moment then ran inside into her room, pouting.

After tending to the horses and washing up and eating they chatted with the women.

Louise declared that her second trunk had come. James, cleared his throat and asked her, "If we put up a curtain to make a bed private, would you come out and stay with us?" his voice trailing off.

"Yes, oh yes, that I would like to," she answered and James simply glowed. That was all he hoped for.

Then Louise broached the question about Amy. "Would it be possible to show her what it is like on the farm. I don't think she has any idea, and we were hoping it would help her to understand what she must do to help."

John spoke up then. He looked doubtful. Carefully he turned away and quietly said, "I don't think Amy is built for this country. I hate to do this but I believe now that she must go back home. I love her, but I am afraid that I can't live the life she wants and vise versa." By the time he finished tears were streaming down his face. Meg rushed to his side with comforting words. She felt so sorry for him, as did Louise and Liz who had painstakingly tried to entice Amy to at least try.

"I am going to build a Soddy with the help of the neighbors and Jim and Bill, if he's better. It is going to take time and a lot of work, and I just can't be trying to run around to keep her happy. I have ordered all the tools and things that I need to build."

Amy came into the room, just as John was finishing. "I don't want to go home, I love you and I want to be with you," as tears continued covered her cheeks smearing her make up.

"All right, Amy, perhaps you should come out with us and see what I mean," he said with emphasis.

"I will get ready for the morning. Will we leave right after breakfast?" asked Amy.

"It will be early in the morning, just after daylight." James added stressing the time. Then looking at Louise, he asked, "Will you be ready to come and stay?" at which Louise nodded.

"I will get you a lunch to take with you and some tea, although it might be a bit cold by the time you stop," said Liz.

"That would be lovely, Liz. We do appreciate it," both men added.

Early next morning, James spoke to Louise, quietly, asking if taking this woman was wise. He felt she did not seem the type that would endure the wagon ride. Louise nodded and put her hand to her mouth until Amy had disappeared into her room, to get her bag to take with her.

"I have no choice, she is determined to come with us," as she grasped James hand. He nodded and drew her close to him for a fleeting moment.

The men left to collect the wagon and supplies and announced they would be back in an hour to pick up the women, warning them not to bring too much, because there would not be a lot of room besides the trunk.

Louise had already packed her bag, which wasn't very big but it was all she had. When Amy finally came out of her room, she had three large suitcases, at which Louise, grimaced and said, "Amy, do you ever listen to what people say? There is not enough room for all of your cases. We are only taking you out for a short time."

"But I must have these things with me," cried Amy. At that, Louise just threw up her hands and sat down to wait. They rose when they heard the wagon coming. After stopping in front of the house, both men came inside to haul the trunk out. "Sorry, Louise, but we can only take one trunk at a time,"

When it was loaded, they motioned to the women to come aboard. When John saw what Amy was carrying, he hesitated, "Sorry, Love, but only one case, if you don't mind?"

Amy sighed and was about to argue, when she saw the loaded wagon, "Oh, my where are we going to sit?" she cried.

"We have made room behind the driver's seat. We take turns driving, so we need to sit up front. Unless of course, you know how to drive a team of horses," added John. At which everyone laughed but not Amy. She looked bound and determined but this time, John, spoke up again. "Amy, if you are going with James and Louise and I, you will mind what we tell you, otherwise you can stay behind." She pouted but got into the wagon with a great to do, and settled beside Louise in the back. The look on her face, told another story.

James called to the horses, and the wagon started to move. At first, the horses were anxious to get going and wanted to run. James gave them their head for a while, then slowed them down when they encountered some ruts. The wagon jiggled and jumped around. Amy cried out loudly at every bump, but Louise kept hushing her and pointing to sit back and relax. Louise was interested in all around her and wanted to memorize every tuft of brush, every rabbit she saw, everything along the way. She tried hard to ignore Amy's constant comments as they rumbled along.

Suddenly, John called a halt to the wagon. James obliged and looked askance. "If you are going to continue to grumble like this, I suggest that we turn around and take you back. I cannot take this anymore. Amy. I suggest you, GO HOME!"

Everyone was startled and James without a word, turned the wagon around. Amy, was stunned and started to cry. She tried to say something, but John was not listening anymore and showed it. She knew at that time, that she had over stayed her welcome and acquiesced, her make up causing her to look extremely funny. Louise, couldn't help but break out laughing, pointing at Amy's face. Tears streaked down her cheeks and lipstick smeared her chin washing it onto her dress. When Amy looked down at her dress, she cried even more and the men at this time started to laugh, shaking their heads.

James spoke up then, " This is no time to be acting childish, I suggest you listen to John. You are just not cut out for this life, I am so sorry," he finished just as the wagon came to a stop in front of Mrs. Long's. Meg and Liz came running out to find out what happened. When they saw the tear streaked face, they knew, she was being sent home. John was looking unhappy.

Amy jumped down from the wagon, turned to John for one last chance, but John looked away and motioned to James to leave saying, "It is getting late; we have lost a lot of time. Please, let's just go." He did not even look back. This was a blow to his ego and left a hole in his heart as well. Both Louise and James, said nothing. They felt a deep empathy towards this young man with such plans for the future. The women had taken Amy by the arm into the house, promising to take care of her.

They continued their way home, as James called it. No one said anything for miles. Soon they found a grassy area in which to stop for lunch and give the horses a drink and a break. Louise quickly got the bag lunch out and put out the tin cups, slices of buttered bread and cheese and slices of meat, along with the tea.

Louise asked James to say the blessing. He agreed and added how sorry he was that Amy did not feel a part of this new country and prayed that John would find someone who would. John only nodded and reached for a cup. A load was lifted off Louise, because she had hoped to change Amy, for John's sake, but it had been taken out of her hands, as if God had intervened.

They continued on their way after a short rest. Louise was lulled by the movement of the wagon and fell asleep often, only to be awakened by a bump as the wagon lurched and rolled along. At last, James announced they were almost home.

"Whoa, he called to the horses and they stopped right in front of the funniest looking house, Louise had ever seen.

"Louise, are you awake, this is to be your new home," James said.

"This is your home?" she said quietly, but in her heart she knew that it was. She had been listening to the folk coming in to see Liz and the customers that she had cut hair for. Well, she would make the best of it and hopped down from the wagon with determination.

"Bless you, Louise, I knew you would understand," James uttered with relief. He had started to call her Louise as did the others.

"I will unhook the horses and look after them. You can show Louise, our pride and joy, " John said as daylight was beginning to fade.

The inside of the shack, wasn't so bad. Louise, noted the curtain that was put up for her, the rough hewn table and benches, a couple of chairs and cots, a small stove with a large kettle sitting on it. She noted the floor was covered with heavy cardboard. The ceiling was covered with some sort of muslin and the walls seemed to be whitewashed.

"I can help you unload," she spoke to James and proceeded to turn around to go outside, but just as she did, someone coughed. It was Bill, and James was checking on him. He looked pale and listless. *I have my work cut out for me.* "James, he is very sick. I will do what I can for him." She had already checked on a doctor and hospital, hearing that Bill was sick.

"We believe, with the Grace of God, he needs some good food and rest. He has worked so hard out here," replied James.

"We will work together to get Bill back on his feet," replied Louise.

Chapter Five

Louise had already decided that the house definitely needed a woman's touch. Her mind was planning what to do with the flour sacks that divided her bed from the rest of the room. There wasn't much to work with, but by golly, she would do her best. She was with James, and that meant a lot. She was curious though, as to how John was going to fare. Would he finish his Soddy now? He seemed a little distracted today. But that was not her problem, he would have to decide what to do.

"What do I do for water?" Louise enquired.

"We get a barrel of water from a spring for drinking and cooking and we have a dug well for washing and other things. We have to keep a lid on the water pail at all times. Jim and John will see to water," Bill replied weakly

"What about wood for the stove?" she asked then remembered that Bill was weak and she shouldn't be asking him these questions, but he answered her.

"Usually, a couple of farmers would hire or take a couple of wagons and travel west of here to wooded areas and pick up trees that have fallen, cut them up and bring them back, or we can order some coal from the coal mines also west of here. Some stoves can use chips or shavings from the sawmills," his voice loosing strength.

Louise took stock of what she had and began to plan her day. First the men would definitely need a cup of tea and whatever she could come up with. She needed to know what supplies they had in store. She found the cupboard was stocked with a few spices and flour and sugars, stored in a covered pail. At that moment James came in and explained to her that the food that needed to be kept cold was in a crockery container, partly buried in the ground on the north side of the house. He took her out to show her that container which held a sealer of milk, a sealer of canned meat, a few eggs, some sausages and James added a package of cheese and butter. He also showed her the shed where they kept the horses. Louise was surprised that they had existed in this way for so long.

"Where do you get milk and eggs?" Louise asked.

"A neighbor comes by once a week on the way to town and sells us milk and eggs if we need any. We, or rather John snares a rabbit every once in a while or a prairie chicken. Bill knows how to skin and prepare the rabbit and we both know how to pluck the chicken, although there is not much meat on them. Often we used them for soup or stew. You will soon see!" James answered to a wide eyed Louise.

James continued to explain. "Louise, I have my work cut out for me. Do you see that stand of wheat? It is growing fast and starting to ripen and then we will have to binder it for selling. John & Bill have been working with me, getting the land broke.

Bill is definitely looking better, but he is not strong enough to help. The house and food are in your hands, my darling. And I can't tell you how pleased I am that you are here. I thank God for sending you," holding her close for a moment.

"God didn't send me, my love for you made me come," she answered annoyed that he didn't kiss her then and there. Then as if, an after-thought, he turned and held her once more kissing her firmly on the lips. She sighed. This is what she was waiting for.

He left abruptly, telling her, that work awaited him. "Bill can answer any questions you may have. I need to see to the horses and talk to John. We will come in shortly for tea."

Louise was left to figure out what to do for tea. Then she remembered the flap cakes and decided that is what she would make, plus she could make a pudding with milk, bread and spices. With that in mind, she went to work and soon there was an aroma of pancakes filling the house. It aroused Bill from his sleepiness and he struggled to get to the table. The smell, he said, made him hungry. He watched Louise as she worked with the stove and the frying pan. The kettle boiling and the clink of dishes and Bill talking brought the other two men hurrying in. They were met with such a pleasant sight and quickly sat around the table.

The next morning, Louise went exploring outside. It was so bare; it fairly took her breath away. Then she noticed some berry bushes outside and the berries tasted rather good, so she thought to make a syrup out of them. When she told the men, they wondered what in the world had she found. James asked her where she found them and when he looked where she pointed, he smiled, "Those are raspberries; good they are just ripening."

Bill spoke up at the moment, when he looked out the door, "Louise, did you leave a pail of water outside?" Louise glanced out as well and before anyone could stop her, she was out the door and screaming, "Get away from there," waving her hands in the air.

James hollered and ran after her, "Louise, stop, stop!" but before he got the words out, the skunk had turned and released its defense, leaving Louise coughing and spitting. She looked at James, dazed. She coughed a few more times before gagging, exclaiming, "Never in all my life, have I smelled anything as horrible as that?"

"That is something you will need to learn in this country. That is a skunk, and his natural defense against predators is just that. They will only do that if threatened, so remember that," adding, "are you feeling okay?" realizing, she looked a little pale.

"Help yourself to the flap cakes, and tea, I am just going to lie down," she announced trying hard to be strong but without much success, adding, "there is so much I have to learn."

The rest sat down at the table and ate heartily, murmuring how good it tasted.

"Jim, she is the best thing, that ever happened to us all, don't ever let her go," said John

"Hallelujah! " shouted Bill. He was actually looking a little better.

James nodded and smiled, "She is the best! And she has always called me, James."

After eating, they joined forces and cleaned up the table, put water on to wash up the plates, cups and cutlery nodding to each other to be quiet while doing this. When finished they quickly left, leaving Louise all alone. Bill joined them outside, saying he needed some fresh air and wanted to talk to them. "In a week, with this good food, I should be feeling better and able to work. John, if you are still going ahead with your house, I wouldn't mind helping. And when the crop is ready, I would like to help harvest. I am looking forward to doing this," his voice fading at the end.

"We would be glad of your help, Bill," said John while James nodded in agreement.

"First the house, then the crop," noted James.

"We start on the house next Monday. That will give you another week to recuperate. I will only let you do light work to begin with," John said.

"Good that's settled then, I see you've rented a tent, John? Are you going to stay over there," asked James?

"Yes, I plan on doing that," he answered adding, "the only thing I need is someone to prepare some food for the crew, probably just lunch?"

"I think, Louie, will look after that. She doesn't know the neighbors. I will visit them and introduce her, although, I think they may have met her in town. She cut a lot of hair." Realizing he still called her Louie, he decided it would sound better if he called her Louise.

"Then I will leave that up to you, Jim or James," They were starting to call him James after listening to Louise.

"Right, I will ask Louie/Louise."

John, then grabbing the reins of his horse, jumped on and rode off.

When asked about the meals for the crew. Louise was spell bound. " What in the world am I going to feed them?" she asked.

"On Sunday afternoon, we usually meet at the neighbors for a short talk on the Bible. We have been talking about building a church soon. Then I will introduce you to some of the neighbor ladies and they will know what to do. It will do you good to get to know them," he held her tight adding, " I still am so glad you are here, I love you," his voice strong.

Humbled, Louise answered, "Of course, I will do what I can."

"Thank you for helping Bill. He is so appreciative and feeling better already." It was times like this, that she felt that strong emotion that had sustained her during her arduous journey to this wild country. She could tell, he loved it here, and knew that it was where they would make their home. It was hard living in the same house, and yet living apart so to speak. But she also knew how James would not compromise the living arrangement. She had wondered if he ever thought of sitting down and reading the Bible any more. Now she knew. She did as well whenever she had a chance. A church, how good that sounded.

When Sunday came, Louise was ready. She had prepared herself for this day and couldn't help feeling excited. She missed the weekly trips to church, the sermons and the camaraderie. and most of all, she missed talking to the ladies. Then she had another brain wave. She would find a way to go to town, as it were, and see Meg and Liz, and visit the General Store. There she would maybe find the pans and bowls; she was looking for.

"I will ask James about it, and maybe we could ask the neighbors today?"

Excitement was building up in Louise. She could hardly wait for James to get the horses and wagon ready Sunday. She thought it was going to be only the two of them, but she was disappointed when Bill, as weak as he was, managed to get up and ready himself. Then John joined the three. "Okay, everyone, lets go. The weather is good right now," said James, as he checked the sky.

"Yeah, let's go," replied John, as he helped Bill into the wagon."

James had placed a chair in the wagon for Louise, but Bill claimed it when he got in so Louise settled herself on a blanket, sitting cross legged. It wasn't that comfortable but she would endure. Her mind wandered as they ambled along the path. It didn't look like much of a road, but did look well travelled. She wondered how many families, lived in this area and was about to ask, when Bill replied as if reading her thoughts.

"There must be a dozen families living in this area, from what I have heard. They would know today at Bannisters."

"Oh, that's the name, I know. I cut the hair for a couple of boys. I met Mrs. Bannister, yes, a lovely woman."

Soon, James was laughing and waving hello, "We are at the Bannisters. I will let you and Bill off at the door, and John and I will see to the horses," as he pulled up.

The Bannisters

The family came out to greet them, including some of the other neighbors. They were anxious to meet them and after the greetings went into the living room. It was a pleasant sight. Louise couldn't help notice the walls, nicely papered and curtains on the windows. The floor seemed to be covered with some sort of tiles, she wasn't quite sure but she was going to ask about it if she got a chance. Bill and Louise were offered a bench to sit on.

Within seconds another wagon arrived with several more adults and children. Then another came right behind. Before long, there were at least four wagons tied up. The men were tending to the horses, as the rest were greeted at the door. It was beginning to be quite a crowd.

The last man to enter was James, and when he came in everyone clapped heartily. This surprised Louise and she looked at James questioningly. He winked at her and began to speak.

"Some of you have met Louise, my betrothed, and some of you have not. She has come all the way from Leeds, England, to be with me," hesitating, he kneeled down in front her saying," Louise, will you be my wife?"

Louise was stunned. Never in all her life, did she expect this, stuttering and stammering she answered, "Yes, of course, I will" She was ecstatic. Clapping and laughter claimed the air, as James escorted her to sit beside him.

James, then turned and addressed the crowd as a minister would. He followed with a Bible verse and then a familiar hymn. They seemed to be perfectly at ease with this show of leadership. Louise couldn't believe her ears. When he told a story to the children, they hung on to every word. *Had he been doing this all the time?* He seemed very collected and she herself got caught up in the singing and mini sermons where other men took turns saying what was in their hearts. At last James asked everyone to pray for a church to be built in this area. "Amen," came loud and clear.

"Tea and cakes will be served outside, since it is such a lovely day," Mrs. Bannister announced. Probably a good idea, with so many people in such a small space. Louise was glad to get out in the fresh air and sought out James, who was talking to some of the men. He spotted her, and came over, catching her hand in his. "James, have you been the leader in this gathering?" she asked.

"I guess, you could say so, some people are shy about talking in public, but I have been in the band at church for so many years, that I believe I know some of the sermons by heart. I just like to keep the idea of a church someday and I think it helps people in this harsh land, to talk to God often."

"I am so proud of you, and when will we be able to get married?"

He anticipated her question and laughed, looking at her, he said," Rev. Lloyd will be here, on July 1, next summer which is 1905, and will marry us," he smiled, adding, "not long from now, my love."

Louise couldn't help smiling, all the rest of the afternoon. Soon it was time for them to leave. Before they left she cornered Mrs. Bannister, " I want to go to town, soon, but I need a ride. If you know of anyone going that has room for me, please let me know,"

Mrs. Bannister nodded and said, "I believe we have to go in sometime this week. You can come with us. It will be a chance to get to know one another."

"Thank you. I would appreciate that."

"It's my way of saying thank you for cutting our hair."

Waving, Louise climbed into the wagon, and this time John motioned for her to take the seat beside James. He sat down beside Bill, smiling and soon both were fast asleep. But not Louise or James, they were busy talking about the future and prayed for a good harvest, so they could afford the wedding. They were both looking forward to it.

The Soddy

Early Monday morning, James had the horses hooked up ready to go, before Louise had breakfast ready. She called to him, to come and eat. "You must have something on your stomach, to keep you going." Bill was already at the table, helping himself to porridge and bread when James said, "Bill, I don't want you to work at John's house yet, maybe you could help Louise, with the lunch. I will send someone to get you."

"Louise are you all right with that?" asked James. She was busy at the stove, making their tea, "yes," she called. She was already thinking of what and how to take the lunch, at least her part. She knew that the other neighbor women would be bringing food as well.

The morning went fast. Louise had Bill busy the whole time. She even found time to trim his unruly hair. Suddenly there was a team of horses standing outside, patiently waiting for them. It caused some excitement among the two, for they were not quite ready. However, the driver never complained. Once they were loaded, he got the team moving. "Glad to have you aboard Miss," he drawled.

The ride was anything but smooth, and Louise worried about the tea, hoping that it would not tip over and spill. She had wrapped it in towels, trying hard to keep it as warm as she could.

Bill questioned her about the pail she insisted on bringing. "Oh, that is for the men to wash up. After all they are handling dirt, and goodness knows what," she said nonchalantly.

Bill nodded, wearing a grin. He should have guessed after helping this woman out around the house. She was always cleaning and washing her hands.

When they arrived all the men stopped and happily put down their load. "What a pleasant sight," said James and John respectively. Other teams were also driving in and parking beside them. Soon there was a bevy of women busy bringing out bowls of food. The aroma was beginning to make them drool. Louise had set her food out at the back of the wagon but held her hand up to wait. She took the pail and left. She had witnessed a creek nearby, the same one that ran by their place, and filled up her pail. Bringing it back she announced, "I would like you to wash your hands and James will say 'Grace' before we eat."

There was hard boiled eggs, biscuits with meat, bread pudding with cream, cookies, small berry tarts, but the biggest hit came from the sausages wrapped in pancakes that Louise had made with the sausages she had found in the crockery. They were the talk of the group, even the women. All crowded around Louise to find out what she had done. "Oh, something I learned from the cook on the wagon train, I came on from Winnipeg," she answered to their questioning looks.

"I am going to try that too," said one of the ladies.

"Me, too," said another.

"My dear, you have made a hit with all these neighbors, today. I am so proud of you," said James quietly so as not to embarrass her.

Before they were even finished, one of the women approached Louise and asked about doing some sewing for her. Louise nodded and told her to call on her as soon as possible and we will talk about it. She added that she was a seamstress, but did not have any material to work with saying, "Perhaps the General Store will order some in."

The women were all ears and soon Louise was inundated with requests. She had made several dates before leaving to go home. Louise wanted to get some work done before James came home. She knew that soon they would call it a day, so the men could go home after making a good start on the Soddy. She had taken a keen interest in what the men were doing noticing where they had dug the bricks out of the sod, to form the floor of the house. It looked like hard work. Interested, she asked one of the men, how they were going to do the walls of the house now they had dug out the sod to form the floor. He told her, after tamping the floor down, they would cut rectangles of sod to be placed side by side for the wall with grass side down for the first row, then up so the roots will grow; then another to be laid crosswise. It will form a very strong wall. Then she had queried about a door as well. He told her it will be built separate with planks and boards and the blocks of sod built around it. And when she asked about windows? He shrugged and said that too comes later. And then before she could ask anything more, he left her standing there saying he had to get back to work.

That made her realize it was getting late and she had many things to do. "Come on Bill, we need to make a mile, isn't that what they say?" Louise laughed.

Next day, Mrs. Bannister called on her and invited her to go to town with them the following week. They would make an early start and be back around midnight or so. The men would just have to fare for themselves that day, but Louise would leave supplies for them. Bill would look after the house unless he went off to help John and James.

The days flew by and soon it was time for her sojourn into town. She was excited to see Liz and find out about Meg and what happened to Amy. The wagon rides didn't bother her any more. Oh, she was always a little stiff the next day but that was all. She could endure most anything now that she knew what was ahead.

Before dawn, Louise was up and getting dressed, when the wagon appeared at the door. She hurried out, closing the door quietly not wanting to bother the men. However, while she was getting aboard James and Bill showed up at the door waving.

The sound of the wagon lured her into nodding every once in a while. She tried so hard to keep listening to Mrs. Bannister, who seemed needing to talk. She was a large woman, with hair the color of honey framing an oval face. She wasn't pretty but her voice was pleasant. Arriving at the rooming house, Liz and Meg were there greeting her before she could get down from the wagon.

"What ever happened with Amy?" Louise wanted to know.

"Amy, went to Saskatoon a couple of days later and we never heard another word from her. Hopefully she went home," added Meg.

"And Meg, how are you?" Louise asked.

Liz spoke up then, saying, "Meg has had bad news, Louise. She doesn't want to talk about it."

"Oh, Meg, I am so sorry. I was going to ask you to help me during the building of John's Soddy. I can just barely keep up with the lunches and all."

Meg had tears running down her face. She just nodded when Liz spoke but now seemed to want to say something.

"My husband, was killed working on the railroad several months ago. The red coats finally located me. I really don't know what I will do. For now, I have been helping Liz for my room and board."

"Would you like to come out with me?" Louise asked again, "It would be such a blessing, and John is working so hard and gets a little depressed at times, but he will not give up. He loves this country and the people. By the way James has proposed and we will be married when Rev. Lloyd comes here in July."

"Oh, Louise, congratulations and yes, I would love that. It will give me a chance to get to know more of the people. Liz has been such a dear, but I need to move on, I know."

"Then that is settled. I am going over to the General Store to order some goods and when I come back, we can have tea. In the meantime, I will ask the Bannister's if we can add one more person to the wagon. You might have to run behind," and they all laughed.

At the General Store, Louise checked everything on her list and more. She had to be careful because she did not know how much room there would be. Hopefully, there would be room for Meg. She was excited. When she got back to Liz's, Meg was no where to be seen.

"Where is Meg, Liz?" Louise asked

"She disappeared some time ago, but she will be back," Liz said reassuringly. At that moment, Meg did arrive, but on horseback. Both women looked askance.

"I know how to ride and I borrowed a horse for a couple of days. I haven't ridden in some time. It will feel good," Meg called.

Mr. Bannister who was tall and thin, with a very pleasant face and bushy beard announced his arrival and told them he had stopped at the General Store for supplies and picked up Louise', so they were ready to leave. However, Liz, called to them to come in for tea and biscuits. Meg tied up her horse and joined them. It was a time of lightness and laughter. Mr. Bannister was funny and had them squealing with laughter. Even Liz, came out from the kitchen to join in the mirth, saying "Jolly good, I have enjoyed you all, please come back and tea is on the house," However, Larry or Mr. Bannister, refused to have it. "I will pay my way, if you don't mind? I too, have enjoyed this afternoon, but we must make a mile, ladies, or the night owls will be hooting us on the way." Again, they all laughed, but before getting on board, Liz called, "I miss you two young women, more than I have ever missed anyone, I have to tell you. Please come back and visit me often."

The trip was uneventful, as Louise chatted with Meg and Mrs. Bannister or Betty as she wished to be called. Meg rode along-side the wagon and Louise could tell she was quite comfortable on a horse. She hoped and prayed that maybe there was a chance that John would notice Meg. She could only hope. But she also realized James would forbid her to interfere.

They stopped briefly to give the horses a drink at a creek they had to cross and Meg did the same for her horse. Soon they were back on their way and Larry let the horses run for a while, slowing up just before Louise' home, where they would part ways, after unloading her supplies.

"Thank you from the bottom of my heart," said Louise and Meg in unison.

James, Bill and John were all there to help unload and welcome the women home.

"Seems you've been gone a long time, even though it is just a day," said James. The other men simply nodded.

John immediately took care of Meg's horse. Louise noted that he had also helped her dismount. She pursed her lips and winked at James. He didn't say anything nor did Bill, but she suspected both had noticed.

It was a wonderful two days the two women had, between putting together lunches and teas they found time to reminisce while working. Bill did odd jobs and kept out of their way sensing they needed that time.

Louise asked Meg about her husband, thinking she could be grieving underneath the façade. However, Meg openly talked about her relationship with him. "I believe, I was fast loosing any feeling toward him, when I did not hear a word. However, when I came, I realized that he probably was the same as James, having a rough time getting word back to me. Now I feel a little guilty thinking that way."

"Do you want to stay?" Louise asked, hoping she would

"I am beginning to like it here, the people are so friendly and accommodating. They have given me a lift but I need a purpose to stay. I have made so many friends and John has been so understanding," she added.

Louise couldn't help feeling that Meg was leaning toward John, as if he was somehow linked to her actually staying. She mentioned him often, and always with a softness. It was apparent that she was falling for this man. *I do hope that he will eventually feel the same, even though it hasn't been that long that he sent his fiancé home.*

"John, may be your answer to the future," Louise quipped.

"Oh, I am sorry, Louise, I shouldn't go on like that," she answered.

"If you feel something for this man, you should let him know. It has been a tremendous let down for him, finding his betrothed so inadequate to be a farmer's wife and so demanding."

"I guess!" Meg answered.

Finally, it was time for Meg to take the horse back to town. Louise was sad to see her go, but hopefully there will be other times. The morning Meg got ready to leave, she was surprised to find John at the door, waiting on his horse and handing the reins to her.

"Oh, how can I thank you, John," Meg cried.

"I thought I would ride along with you. I need to order more supplies and we are taking a day off from the building, to give the men a well earned rest. *Did he do this on purpose knowing that Meg was leaving?*

"Have a good ride, both of you. John, we will meet you again in two days," called James as all waved to the two.

"I wonder," said James.

Louise didn't learn about their day until well after when Meg told her in detail what happened.

The ride started out uneventful for the first part of the morning. The sun was shining and a little breeze kept the mosquitos away. After some time riding, John suggested that we stop and let the horses have a drink at the creek on the way and so we did. He was such a gentleman.

We stopped to have the lunch you packed for us and found a nice grassy spot to sit on the side of the creek and tethered the horses to graze. It was calm and so peaceful as we opened the package you gave us and to our delight, it was those sausages wrapped in pancakes. We laughed and ate and talked about the last two days.

Then John asked about my husband. He was so sorry. It had been on his mind for some time. He desperately wanted to know how I was feeling. Without hesitation, I understood and gave him my story and how I was confused as to what to do next. I told him, I could stay at Mrs. Long's but that's not a future and when I sighed John reached out and cupped my hand and when he touched me an electric shock went through my body and I reacted. John thought he had done something wrong and recoiled. I tried to tell him but started crying and he held me so close, I didn't want to move.

Then out of the blue, an arrow came whizzing by. Immediately John jumped up and grabbed me. I froze, unable to move, but he helped me get on my horse and jumped on his and we were off at a fast pace. Thank goodness the horses were rested and ready to race. Another arrow whizzed by as we rode down the road but as we rounded a bend, we saw two redcoats.

One of them turned, slowed and shouted, that they were on their way to see the chief of these renegades. They have been harassing some of the farmers in this area and need to be stopped. They didn't think they wanted to hurt us, just scare us and told us to carry on. I was still shaking when we got to Liz's, I couldn't even go pay for my horse.

Liz couldn't wait to hear what had happened. She sensed it when I jumped down off my horse and ran up the stairs, out of breath and talking wildly. She was not surprised because she had heard the stories of harassment and theft by the two young bucks. She told me, that those two, were renegades and the chief was not a war-monger. He would discipline them. The Redcoats told us they would find out what is going on and there were more redcoats coming. When I heard that, I felt better and waited for John to come back so I could tell him.

I told Liz how grateful I was for John but I know she already guessed because she just smiled and motioned me to sit down and have some tea.

When John came back and saw the two of us smiling, he joined us, asking what was going on? We told him and he relaxed. It had been quite a ride. When he was leaving, John motioned to me to come outside for a moment. He asked me if I would mind if he came to see me now and again? You know what I said, don't you Louise? Because the day was almost gone and he hadn't got his supplies ordered, he decided to stay overnight. I was excited and told him I would serve him supper that night. Of course Liz said laughing, he could stay but in a separate bedroom.

That night, Louise, I had a hard time getting to sleep, especially with John in the next room. I hadn't felt like this in a long time. It was hard to keep from smiling but then, guilt would claim my thoughts and I would lie there trying to justify my emotions. Was this right? I have not been widowed for long, what will they think of me? The thoughts whirled around in my head until I drifted off. In the morning, after getting dressed and going to the kitchen to help Liz, I knew how I looked, but duty calls. Liz sensed my turmoil and talked to me over a cup of tea.

She knew what I was concerned about, and told me that I did not ask to be a widow, but sometimes things happen and there is nothing we can do about it. She also said 'I know what Louise would say, pray and he will show you the way. Now, cheer up remember he has not had it easy either. I believe that you will make that man very happy and I thank you. Don't beat yourself up! You have a right to be happy, and that is all she would say except we love you.

I thanked her, and I thank you for listening to me. That is what happened on that day I left your place with John. I know you have heard stories, but that Louise is my story."

Chapter Six

At the farm, Bill and James were looking at the binder they had bought. The grain was getting riper by the day and they planned to use it soon. However, the canvas didn't look so good. They decided it had to be repaired before they could use it. Both men went to the house, each silent. Louise noted the expression on both faces.

"What in the world is wrong? You two look like doomsday has come."

"Our binder canvas has a slit in it and we don't know how to repair it," replied James.

"How heavy is the canvas?" asked Louise.

"I don't really know," replied Bill.

"Since my sewing machine is a heavy duty one, could I try to mend the tear?"

With that statement, both men looked stunned. Neither had thought about Louise and her sewing machine. Indeed, it was a heavy one but they were still a bit reluctant to even try.

"If you can get the canvas free, bring it to me. I will do my best to repair it," At that point both men jumped into action. They would try to release the canvas. They both had a doubtful look on their faces, though, which made Louise laugh.

"Let's give it a try," she said with emphasis.

"Let's pray it works," said Bill, who wore a more anxious look.

It took the men quite a time to get the canvas released from its rollers, but they finally succeeded. By this time Louise had her sewing machine ready to go. Thankfully the sewing company had added extra heavy needles and thread, which made her wonder. *Did they know something about this country all along?*

While Bill proceeded to put supper out, which Louise had left on the stove. She had set one half of the table and the other half with her sewing machine so she could start as soon as they ate. When the men washed up and sat down, Louise was the one who said grace. "Father, bless this food and James and Bill and please let me do the repairs that they need, Amen," as both men smiled broadly.

Right after they ate, both men cleaned up the table and washed the dishes, leaving Louise to work on the canvas. It was dusty and dirty, but she ignored that. She tackled the job, like she would tackle any job, with gusto. Trying different ways and struggling with the unruly stuff, she finally got it where she could start to sew, zigzagging along the tear. When she was satisfied it would hold firm, she announced the job was done.

Both men were ecstatic. James hugged her, while Bill clapped his hands. They picked up the canvas and were out the door before Louise could get off her bench. She was happy, because they were happy. She didn't quite understand how important that little gesture was until she watched them reinstalling the canvas and studied the machine, asking questions all the while. James explained to her the procedure as he worked. Bill finished it by telling her after they cut the grain, it would be tied and left in bundles or sheaves that they would have to stook. "Stook?" Louise asked, with a funny look on her face, that made both men laugh.

John came riding into the yard at that moment and saw them talking and laughing and wanted to know what was going on. Bill explained what had transpired and finished by saying,

"That woman is one blessed woman."

"I have found me one, too" John exclaimed when he jumped down.

Everyone looked questioningly at him. "Who," they said in unison.

"Oh, just some girl, I met," he answered.

"I know it's Meg," cried Louise.

"Yes," replied John as he leaped back on his horse and rode off. He already knew that the harvest would be paramount and his house would be put on hold.

"Wow, an end to a very blessed day," said James adding "Thanks to God and to Louise, for making it so."

The cutting was started the very next day and continued until all the grain was cut and bound into sheaves. It was exciting to watch as the horses pulled the binder around and around the acres of grain. Louise was mesmerized by the whole operation.

Next came what they called stooking. They would be stooking the tied sheaves, five would be placed upright with grain at the top, leaning against one another to stay standing, so that any moisture would run off and they would dry out quickly. That was one place, Louise thought she might help, but James refused to let her even try. He told her it was a man's work and they needed her in the kitchen, after all food is important too.

"We have a good crop, this year and should get a good price for it," Bill added.

"We will divide it into three, and that should give us all a good start for next year," continued James.

"I will be moving on, James, I think it is time. I plan to work for Mrs. Long. I believe she needs someone to look after some of the ongoing repairs," said Bill. It was not a big surprise to Louise and James. They had anticipated this might happen. He had spent several days in town during the last month and though he was feeling much better they noticed he still tired easily. Both thought that his idea to help Liz, was a good one.

Now for the threshing, Louise was informed that in approximately three weeks a threshing crew would come with a steam engine and teams of horses and racks would gather the stooks. Then pitch them into a container that would move them onto a conveyor belt and into a hopper that would chop the grain up. The grain would be funnelled into wagons and the straw would be blown out onto a stack. The wagons would then take the grain to a silo for inspection and payment. If the inspection was good, they would receive the top payment. It was the most excitement Louise had felt since her proposal. She scurried around planning, cooking and preparing for the onslaught of men to be fed who would be dusty and tired but very, very hungry.

When the steam machine arrived, anticipation filled the air as the neighbors came with their teams of horses, pulling racks or wagons. The engine started up with a bang, spooking John's team. The horses took off, with John hanging on for dear life. He couldn't stop them. Suddenly they hit some rough ground and the wagon flipped over. John was flung from the wagon, with his hand still entwined in the reins. He was pulled several minutes, before he managed to get loose. The team was long gone, dragging the tongue and leaving the broken wagon behind. John lay inert on the ground. One of the men who was racing after them, loaded him on his wagon and rushed back to the house.

Louise shouted, "Bring him in here and put him on my bed, the women will take care of him." He was laid on her bed, dirty and covered in bits of grass and straw packed with dirt. Mrs. Bannister and some other neighborhood women who had come to help Louise, kept working but watched closely. Louise, quickly got a basin of water and carefully washed his face and hands, which were scratched and bloody. His clothes were in tatters, beyond mending, but they could be replaced. As they were trying to figure out what to do, Meg, who had come to help as well, came flying in, and realizing that there had been an accident, called out. "Who got hurt, not John?"

"Yes, Meg, right now he is unconscious. We don't know the extent of his injuries. Perhaps if he wakes up--." Louise' voice trailed off.

Meg rushed to him and kneeling beside him, cried, "Oh, don't leave me now, John. I want to spend more time with you," Then as if he heard her, he moaned. Quickly, Meg, cupped his head and kissed his lips, not caring who was watching. "We need help; - I am going for help. The Post Office at Wirral will get word to the Doctor who comes occasionally, "said Meg.

Bill came in just then and hearing Meg's last statement exclaimed, "No, Meg, I will go, I can ride your horse, you stay with John," and with that he dashed out the door but was stopped by the men. James was calling and motioning to him, "The first wagon of grain is ready to leave, could we take John in by cushioning him on top of the grain?"

"Yes," cried Meg. I can ride beside the wagon. "Is Bill driving the wagon?"

"We hoped he would, that would help us here."

During the movement of getting him settled, John had regained consciousness, but seemed dazed. His arm was giving him trouble and Meg had very gently wrapped a towel around it. She felt that it may be broken. His hand was bloodied and scratched. Louise had washed most of the blood off, but it was still bleeding. Louise wrapped another towel tightly around his hand and placed a blanket on the load to lay him on. As soon as he was ready, the wagon took off slowly at first, then picked up speed, with Meg riding close beside.

Outside, the men had recaptured the runaway team and brought them back and tied them up. The wagon was not fit to use. James had organized the remaining crew and the steam engine continued to puff away.

Louise looked outside and saw the racks were still lining up to the thresher. She shook her head and thought that maybe everything would have come to a standstill, but no. When she asked James that night after supper he said, "Time is of the essence now. The weather is just right and there was naught that we could do for John. We left that to you women, who we knew would deal with it. The crew are anxious to keep going as we will be moving on as soon as we are finished here. They haven't forgotten John. I asked Bill to help if he could and he said he would and one of the men said he would see about repairing the wagon. We need all the wagons we can get and I actually wanted Bill on that wagon. I will continue to pray for John and for Meg," as he started nodding off.

Louise recognized how tired he was and suggested he go to bed, she still had some work to do for tomorrows meals. She kissed him on the cheek and left him to retire. She felt so thankful to the women of the neighborhood, who continued to prepare food when the accident happened.

It had been such a joy to see these burly men eat heartedly, laughing and jostling one another, during the previous breakfast. James and Bill had joined right in and seemed to enjoy every minute. And speaking of minutes, none was wasted either for as soon as they finished they were back at work, each tending to his own team. Louise noted that it was precision work and when one finished another filled the spot. She had never seen such a camaraderie amongst the neighbors, how wonderful was that.

They learned John regained consciousness and became more alert on the way to town, often moaning if the wagon hit a rough spot. Meg, bless her, calmed him along the way, silently praying that he would be okay. She explained to Louise that when they reached Liz's, as if they already knew, two men were right there to lift John off the wagon and carry him into the house. Liz must have seen them coming because she had a room prepared for him. I rode on to the stables before rushing back to the house.

The Doctor arrived the next day. John had had a very uncomfortable night, often groaning loudly. The doctor determined that he did not have a broken arm but instead his shoulder was dislodged and when he corrected it, we heard him scream. The doctor explained what he did, and after a few moments, John settled down and actually smiled. The doctor continued to say, that he was very bruised and scratched, especially his right hand which he disinfected and bandaged. He also said John is strong and would be up soon but as for his clothes, I cannot mend. Then he sat down to have tea.

"I thanked him and offered to pay him," said Meg.

"No need, young lady, look after him for a couple of days, but don't spoil him too much, now mind," he told me.

"I liked him. He was short and heavy set, with jolly eyes and ruddy complexion and spoke with a slight accent, maybe Scottish, but I never thought to ask his name, "she added.

During this time Bill had emptied the wagon, stopped long enough to check on John, and headed back to the farm where he spoke briefly to Louise. He said," Meg is staying with Liz while John rests. She thought he would be restless and want to get back to the farm but she would try and keep him there for another day just to make sure he was okay."

On the second day, John was up and dressed and waiting, long before anyone else. That did not surprise Liz though and she anticipated such and was prepared. She had tea ready and told him to sit and she would make him breakfast. He was adamant in catching the next wagon going back after depositing the wheat and he wanted to talk to Meg.

The harvesting continued. James was away working at the neighbors, every day, coming home so tired. Louise wanted to go with him and help but he suggested that she help at one or two of the closest neighbors only. Louise wanted to do this to learn some of their secrets for the winter. She had been hearing stories of being snowed in for weeks and she worried about it. They still weren't married and that would not sit well with James, especially if they were alone. She knew from her work how tongues would wag. She may have to move into Liz's for the winter, if Bill decided to leave and John stayed at his own place. She would have to talk with James about this. She also had questions about keeping food safe, and preserving. She hadn't done any of that and needed to know more. There were more berries to pick and she needed to know what to do to preserve them. The neighbors had been there for some time and seemed to be able to survive here, in this treeless land. She had to plan, and perhaps on the weekend when they went to church, she would inquire. For as much as the harvest needed to continue, they insisted on stopping long enough for prayers and Bible readings and tea.

"Yes, I must talk to the women," she chatted to herself. She felt very much alone. She did not have Bill to nurse or John coming and going and activity around the farm that would keep her interest. She found the little patch of garden that Bill had planted, weeded and hoed it. Potatoes and onions were growing nicely and that was about all that she recognized. At least they would have potatoes for winter, but where to keep them. It kept her awake at night thinking about it. Then she remembered her promise to write home.

Dear Mother, Father & Jimmy:

I miss you all, so much. It is difficult to explain where I am and what I am doing. I can look out of the house, such as it is, and see for miles and miles. I watch the horizon regularly for a sign of smoke or storm clouds coming. You have never witnessed a storm like they have here. First you see lightning streak across the boundless sky then the thunder claps so loud, it makes you shudder and then the rain – it just pours down in torrents. And you wait patiently for it to stop, or watch fervently hoping there is no hail in that cloud. For that could be devastating especially at this time of year when the grain is mature.

But, the people, Dad, you would just love them. They are helpful and friendly and I(we) could not survive without them. I currently am living at the farm with three men, oh they are very careful and have curtained off a bed for me. Thanks to Mom for those desiccated soups, I have nursed, Bill, one of James partners, back to health, and John another partner, has just filed his own papers on adjoining land. The winter they tell me can be harsh and we must be prepared. So, I will close now and tell you I am fine and we will be married on July 1, next year. Do wish us well. My love to all of you, Mom, Dad, Jimmy. God Bless you all.

Yours forever,

Louise

As she finished the letter, the tears were streaming down her face. In one year, there had been so many hardships and changes in life and what was in store she did not know. After a cup of tea and a biscuit, she felt better and decided, to try something.

She thought maybe they could build a root cellar; the ladies had been talking about such a thing. Studying the surrounding area, she determined that the most probable place would be in a small hill west of the house which would be easy to get to in winter. Taking a shovel, she attempted to dig into the soil but couldn't penetrate it; it was so hard. She tried again and again, unsuccessful in each attempt. At last she gave up and sat down on a nearby old rickety chair, that someone had left a long time ago.

"Someone lived here at one time," she spoke out loud, not hearing Bill striding up behind her.

"You are right, someone did live here at one time, but we don't know who." Startled she turned and gasped, not expecting anyone.

"Bill, I didn't hear you coming, whatever are you doing here?"

"Did thou miss me?" Bill answered laughing.

"I did, it has been lonely, this last while," she admitted.

"What were you trying to do?" he asked.

"I had an idea, that maybe, and don't laugh, we could build a root cellar. The ladies were saying that is the way to go for winter storage if you don't have a cellar."

"You are right, but the ground here is not ideal for that. If you dig down, say five feet, water will fill your cavity. You see the water level here is high. Believe me we have thought about that. Now since I am moving into Liz's, um Mrs. Long's, I need to pack up my belongings and free up some space for Jim uh James," he said still smiling.

"You are in a happy mood, what is happening?" Louise suspected there was news and she wanted news, any kind of news. "Come, I'll make us a cup of tea and I have some fresh bread and jam, I might add."

"With pleasure, Liz, um Mrs. Long, sure misses your baking back at the eatery."

"Well, I would like to ask you something, I have been mulling over for a while,"

"Go ahead," he said as he sipped his tea and buttered the bread, he couldn't wait to eat.

"Well with you gone and John at his own place, it leaves just James and I, and I know that will not sit well with James at all. We are not married and he is pretty strong minded about that and the tongues will wag."

"I know what you mean," he said between bites. "This is sure good, Louise. I think you need to talk to James about it. He may have a solution to your dilemma."

"Yes, I know you are right, but he had been so tired, I haven't the heart to burden him at this time," she said sighing.

"The harvesting will be done very soon, they are predicting snow, did you know?'

"So soon, I haven't dug up those potatoes you planted or the onions," she answered quickly.

"Let me help you with that, between us we can do it in no time," and with that he gobbled down the last bite and stood up. "Come on, woman, lets do this," and off the two went leaving the cups on the table, which was not Louise' custom. But the thought of snow, woke up a response in her.

James took a good look at them when he came onto the yard, and hollered, "What in the world have you two been up to?" smiling as he called.

"Take a look, and you'll know," cried Louise.

For once the atmosphere was light and fun. James seemed to be in different mood. *There had to be a reason for this.*

"We have finished the harvesting for this year. It looks like it was a good one, and I am ever so thankful we have had good weather. I can now concentrate on getting ready for winter. Still lots to do."

"Bill, are you going to be here or are you moving into town?"

"Yes, I came out to pick up my belongings, but felt I had to stop and help your girlfriend with her harvesting," he said with a laugh.

"Okay, I wanted to know, so I can plan. I believe John will stay with me for the winter and Louise can move into Liz's, until we're married. I believe that would be acceptable around here. What do you think?"

"Do you mean you and John would be here all alone during the winter?" asked Louise a little concerned.

"We would be fine, with a little help from you in the cooking line. I plan on doing some wood work and I think John has some ideas as well."

"Sounds like an excellent plan to me," remarked Bill.

"Louise, we could take your sewing machine in town and your hair cutting supplies. I am sure you will have plenty to do. I chatted with Liz last time I saw her and she is willing to make room in a bedroom down stairs for your machine, so you can have some privacy. I can pay her for it. And I believe Bill has already made his plans for the winter, right?"

"Yes, I have, and I have also made arrangements to stay in town, but not at Liz's. She has promised to marry me in the spring at the same time as you and John," he answered with a wide grin.

"Oh, wonderful, God is looking down on us all, favourably," said James.

Bill left then as John returned and shortly after through yawns and goodnights all went to their separate beds, but not before James hugged Louise, and kissed her on the cheek to which Louise pursed her lips. *He could have kissed me on the lips. Just wait until we are married, then I will show him how to be romantic.*

Chapter Seven

The days flew by, then one morning, when Louise got up and looked outside she couldn't believe her eyes. Everything was covered in a white blanket. It was amazing how pristine it was and how it covered every little item covering it completely. She felt like she wanted to walk in it, just to feel it. *Is that how every child feels when they first see it?* Excited she called to the two men, to hurry up and see this. James and John, yawned and cried at once, "We've seen it before, Louise," slowly getting themselves out of bed. James was mesmerized by the look on Louise' face. He hadn't seen her this excited since he proposed. She reminded him of a little girl, just finding a Christmas present. He knew she would soon find it cold and rather a grind putting on heavier clothes so one didn't freeze and the wind blowing for more than a day.

"Enjoy the day, Louise, it will soon change," he called but she didn't answer.

Suddenly they were interrupted by a scream from Louise. She came running back into the house hollering, "Milk, butter, salt pork, everything is all gone."

"Calm down, Louise. You mean our crock is empty?"

"Yes everything gone!"

"Natives have been here, looks like," sighed John.

"Okay Louise, we will let the neighbors know, so they can watch. It's not the first time they have taken food. Hunting must not be too good for them lately. We will get more milk. You have lots of other food inside that will sustain us."

After the men left to do chores, Louise continued packing still very agitated, thinking, if they asked I would have given them food. Now I will have to make sure all their food is safe.

"Surely they won't come inside," she said aloud, looking at the canned sealers that she had already preserved for the men while she was gone.

When Louise looked outside she was amazed that the snow had disappeared so soon and so completely. The sun was streaming down, leaving small puddles everywhere. Preparing tea, she was lost in her own thoughts, still upset, when John spoke to her.

"I think you and Meg will enjoy the winter in our town. It can be very lonely out here, especially when it snows for days. The wind will make snow drifts as high as this house and make the roads impassible for some time. Us men find projects that we could do during this time, but last winter we ran out of food and that's when Bill started going down hill. We were drifted in for weeks, finally James and I decided to try to get through with one horse. That was the time, James wrote you. He was desperate and so was I and we worried about Bill, having to leave him alone during this time. You were God sent, believe me. James was ecstatic when he heard from the minister in Winnipeg that you were coming."

"I am glad, that I did, <u>also</u> that I was able to help Bill. I will <u>also</u> make sure you have enough food during this winter. I have packed up all my sewing items and my personal items, *belongings* so I can move into town as soon as possible. What about Meg? She must be in town?"

"Yes, she is and is looking forward to spending time with you."

"Good, we will plan our weddings," she said suddenly smiling,

John nodded and laughed as James joined them and learned what was going on.

"Louise, the time has come, we will take you into town tomorrow, if you are ready," he said in the tone of more like I have to, whether I like it or not.

The Move

The move went smoothly, boxes of clothes, cloth, pins etc. went along with the sewing machine and of course the hair clippers and scissors. The wagon was full. The two men loaded the wagon, then John took off on his horse, back to his place. He needed to do some work before winter arrived for good, he told them. But Louise guessed he wanted to leave them alone on the drive. He was a thoughtful person. Louise was happy for the time with James. They had not been alone much of late and needed to talk.

"We will be all right, Louise, if you will help us by baking some bread and making us some food from time to time. I will miss you so much but I am looking forward to getting married come July. By then we should have the crop sowed and some improvements to the house, you will see. I have some projects for the winter in mind, same as John."

"I am also looking forward to July. Meg and I will be planning the wedding and our outfits, my sewing machine has come in handy. I know that we will be joined by Bill and Liz as well, did you know that?" she looked at him with a smile and that, 'I love you' look.

"I had a feeling there was something, promoting the move in Bill's mind. I never thought of Liz, though. That's God way of working isn't it?"

"Yes, it is and I love the idea of a church soon and also a school."

"What a wonderful idea, I will pursue that next meeting, thank you. I never thought of a school, but of course, if we have children. " He looked at her and leaned over and kissed her on the lips, lingering there for some time, until the horses started to trot. Then he laughed heartily and Louise joined in. By the time they got to town, they were in quite a happy mood.

Bill met them at the house and helped unload the wagon, saying, "I hope you don't move too often, it seems to me that your load has increased ten-fold," making them laugh.

"Well, we have a wedding to plan, and I have several projects that need finishing, plus I intend to keep cutting hair," Louise said with enthusiasm.

"Fantastic, come right in, I have a room ready. Meg and I could use some help as well. We have been busy this fall with more people coming all the time," Liz called from the kitchen.

James settled all Louise's belongings in the bedroom and then after clinging to Louise for some time, kissed her again and returned to the wagon without saying much other than, "See you soon, Love."

She watched him from the doorway, until he was out of sight. Sighing, as she returned to the bedroom to unload her clothes and things. Liz had put a table in the bedroom for her sewing machine, with space for attachments etc. A single bed with a pale yellow bedspread, was positioned against one wall, with a chest of drawers and a small mirror, a small table with a pitcher and bowl next to it. One window, facing south, behind her machine, meant good light for sewing. The only other furniture was a large chair, which she needed. Meg's room was right next door only half the size, with a single bed, chest of drawers and stand for a bowl and pitcher and of course a mirror.

Two weeks went by, very fast. Louise sewed as long as the light held, and at night she would tat some lace for their wedding dresses. In between times, she helped out in the kitchen, asking questions about winter all the time. Meg joined Louise when she wasn't sewing. She seemed to get tired of late and Louise and Liz were concerned about it.

Then one morning, she didn't come out for breakfast. Louise decided to knock on her door. When she didn't hear an answer, she carefully opened it to find Meg sprawled on the bed crying. She was in pain and when Louise went closer, she could see blood spatters on the bedspread.

"Meg, what is wrong. You are bleeding?"

"I'm sorry, Louise, I am in a lot of pain right now, yes I am bleeding," she said with extreme anguish.

Louise ran for Liz and between them they got Meg straightened out. Liz knew immediately what was wrong and told Louise to get towels and some hot water. Louise reacted quickly, with her brow wrinkled in question. Liz followed her saying, "Meg is losing her baby. I hope the bleeding stops otherwise, she will bleed to death," she whispered.

"Oh my, I pray she doesn't,"

"Pray hard, my dear for this is not the first one I have seen,"

"Let's get her comfortable, feet elevated and hope for the best,"

The next two hours were tense, as the women sat on each side of the bed. Louise, sat in prayer most of the time. The moaning lasted quite a while until Meg fell asleep from exhaustion. When Liz checked the sheets, the bleeding seemed to have eased and she noted the fetus blob laying on the sheet. She checked Meg's pulse and it seemed to be regular. Both women tried to wake her. Louise massaged her arms and spoke softly to her," Please, Meg, open your eyes, just for a minute," She kept repeating it until she saw one eyelid flutter. It was as if, she was trying hard to open them. All of a sudden, both eyes flew open and she started to cry.

'It's okay, Meg, don't worry, this happens to lots of women," Liz said adding, "Meg, we are going to clean you up, so you can rest."

"I am so sorry, I didn't mean to cause trouble, what will John think of me?"

"If he loves you, like we believe, he will be more concerned about your health and probably sorry for causing this," Liz said adding, "You could have bled to death but you are healthy and strong, so your body has reacted and the bleeding has stopped. You must however, take it easy for a day or two."

"I am going to get you a cup of tea and a biscuit, because you have not eaten today," said Louise as she exited the bedroom.

"No one has been around this morning, so no one will know," mumbled Liz.

Louise and Liz both went to the kitchen lost in their own thoughts.

"I thank the Lord, that Meg didn't bleed to death. I will talk to John about it. He will be devastated to say the least," Louise reiterated.

"Yes, we need to thank God, it was pretty tense there for a while, I thought at one time we were going to lose her. She seemed to give up. Thank you Louise for continuing to talk to her. We will have to keep her in bed for a few days, just to make sure she doesn't start bleeding again. Now take her tea and talk to her. Then she needs to rest," said Liz.

The look on their faces told the story of an intense time. And now it was a waiting game. Both women were exhausted and yet hesitated to leave Meg alone for long.

"We need a doctor in this area, don't we?" Liz said.

"Yes, and we need a doctor to tend to our hurts and we need a church with all the people coming to the west." answered Louise

The next two days passed and Meg gradually gained her strength. On the third day, a doctor did arrive and saw her. He told them they had done well and that she was on the mend, but she must take it easy for some time so the body can heal. Her mental state was in question so she would need help.

After the Doctor left, John showed up. When he heard the story, he was beside himself, swearing softly under his breath. He wanted to see Meg immediately and the women showed him to her bedroom. She was sitting up and when she saw him, she started to cry. At once, he took her in his arms and held her until the sobs subsided.

"I am so sorry, John," she mumbled.

"Shush, it is as much my fault as yours, I am just so glad you are all right," he said with intensity.

"I am going to be fine. The Doctor gave me a good going over and a good talking to. He said I overdid it and I didn't argue."

When John came out, Louise asked," Did James come with you?"

"No, he is coming tomorrow. He wanted to finish up with some building."

Louise was beside herself. Her thoughts ran amok the whole day. *Is he getting tired of me already? I just need a hug. I miss him so!* She sighed as she readied her sewing machine. She planned on sewing in the afternoon, finishing up some work she had contracted from the neighbors. However, she ended up dropping her head in prayer and sitting that way for some time. The days seemed long for her, without the constant worrying about meals and what to do next.

James did finally come in. His face showed his desire, moaning as he held her.

"Louie, oh how I miss you," his voice was low and almost incoherent. "I miss you too, and I worry about you and John out there, "she whispered in his ear.

"Tell me about Meg, John was beside himself, for letting that happen. He spent most of the night in misery. We talked and talked and I finally got him to rest."

"Meg is fine and we had quite a time calming her down. She blamed herself as well. She is doing fine now. Come, I will get you some dinner. You must be starving,"

"Louise, you have done wonders out there, we haven't been starving at all. In fact, we are well fed. The neighbors butchered and gave us a roast of beef. It lasted almost a week and another gave us a chicken to roast and eggs as well. They are wonderful people and I really want to start planning for a church."

With that in mind, both sat down to eat, with a satisfied look, one that didn't go unnoticed. Liz, came and sat down with them, and hearing just the last of the sentence, wanted to know more. When James explained what he was planning and the added idea of a school, she clapped him on the shoulder saying, "That's what I want to hear. We'll build this town up yet. More people are expected in the spring. I am hoping that we can lure a doctor and school teacher here, but we have to work on it.

"The people will make that difference. There are some wonderful people in the country, who have needs and we must promote that, not only that there are people needing a doctor and soon," said James with emphasis.

"Do you know someone who needs a doctor?" she asked knowing that look when he spoke about a doctor.

"Yes, one of our neighbors, told me that he is thinking of quitting farming and packing it up and leaving. His wife is sickly and seems to be getting worse. When will the doctor be coming again? He sounded very anxious."

"Is that the man that came in here yesterday asking about a doctor? He didn't say why or anything else, just asked. We told him that he would be back in a month. Then he just left, without saying who he was and seemed to be in an awful hurry," Louise asked.

"Yes, I am sure that is Ian Taylor who is from Scotland. They have two children. He said his wife has not been well for some time and was slowly going downhill. He is quite worried."

"We can try and send word to the Post Office at Wirral to get word for the doctor to come sooner. Can you get word to Ian if we can do this?"

"I will try my best, and pray for the man at the same time,"

James left but not before hugging Louise and promising to be back again before the winter got too harsh. After he left, Liz and Louise wrote a letter to the doctor, telling him there was an urgent case near Wirral.

The days flew by. They prayed every evening for an answer to their letter, but they knew that it would take time. Liz noted that there were several more people that needed a doctor.

In the meantime, Louise kept on sewing. She was designing a dress for Meg, one for Liz and herself. Material had arrived, plus tiny pearl buttons.

Doctor Arrives

The doctor arrived in town three weeks later. A number of people had made the trip in to see him including Ian, his wife and two children. After their consultation, Ian looked miserable.

Louise invited them in for tea and biscuits but Ian refused. She didn't realize at the moment the reason for his refusal, but he took her aside and told her he did not have the money to spend on both the doctor and lunch. Louise quickly assured him, this was on the house and he should not feel obligated to pay. The children looked hungry, which made Louise feel terrible and needing to do something for the family.

"Come, join me in some lunch, and please tell me what the doctor said," she asked. Ian's wife began to cry. "I have TB, the doctor said and Ian and the children are to be tested as well. He wants me to go to a Sanitarium for a year or two, but I refused. I can't leave my husband and children alone."

Louise thought about what she said, not knowing too much about TB, but was determined to find out.

When Ian and his wife and family left, Louise felt very sad. He had already expressed to James that he thought of leaving and going down east. Probably a good decision, but those poor children needed looking after. She feared that they may all have the disease for they looked pale and thin.

When Doctor Taylor came out of his room for supper, Louise asked him to explain the disease to her. He said Mrs. Taylor had all the symptoms, thin, pale, coughing, chest pains, sometime coughing blood, weak and she could have transmitted it to her husband and children, who also had symptoms. He was worried about them. He gave them some medicine, but did not have any hope of any of them surviving the winter. This all made Louise very sad and it underlined the need for a doctor full time. She made a pact with herself to fight for a church, school, and doctor for the very near future.

A week after the doctor's visit, the weather turned cold with blowing snow. Nobody went outside, unless it was to go to the outhouse.

Louise often thought of those children. It was a rough, tough world, this prairie existence. The snow and cold kept up for almost a month. She hadn't seen John or James and felt that they were trapped. The snow was building up drifting against the house. Bill was forever shoveling the path only to have it drift in again. She continued to sew or tat lace for their dresses. Sewing was often difficult because of the lighting. The sun never shone for days on end. Nerves were getting a little frazzled by the end of three weeks. Meg was back working in the kitchen which wasn't busy, except when some of the people nearby came in to chat. The main topic was always the weather.

Then suddenly a break, the morning dawning clear and bright. It was difficult looking at the snow, it gleamed so bright. Everyone was laughing and going on about the weather's change-ability. There was life all around. Louise prayed that the men would be able to get out and they did with some difficulty, but brought bad news.

"We went over to Ian's to see how they were getting on and his wife had died. He had wrapped her in a blanket and left her on the porch. Their little girl was not looking good at all. Not only that, Ian wasn't very good himself and he worried about their son, who, was also looking pale. He asked me for prayers and to please bury them on their farm and gave me the name of relations in Scotland to be notified. We took some soup that you had canned for us and some of the rest of the bread. I think they were too far gone, though. Mrs. Bannister was going over too and one other neighbor. We are trying to keep in touch with them. I promised to have a funeral for them in the spring. We believed he had resigned himself to their lot. It is so sad. John and I cried and we prayed for them," finished James.

"James, are you and John okay? I don't want you two to get sick as well. I hope you were careful while you were there." Louise asked concerned.

Meg, too was concerned for their welfare and expressed it loudly.

While they were talking and drinking tea, a man suddenly burst into the room.

He asked if there was a James there and when James spoke up, he said, "We need you to come as soon as possible. Ian's taken a turn for the worse, and his children are both very ill. We don't think they will survive the week. He is asking for you, Jim," he said, breathlessly.

"Of course, I will come. John and I will find fresh horses and leave immediately, but you must rest. Your horse will be looked after. Mrs. Long will take care of you."

"Let's go John, before the light fades."

"Oh, do take care, John. Perhaps us women should go as well," Meg added.

"No, I don't want you two out, the weather today is good but it may not last, plus we don't want you exposed to the disease, we need you to pray for these people,"

"We will prepare some food for you to take with you, while you are getting your horses," Louise was already in the kitchen along with Liz and Meg, gathering bread and soup, and other goodies. They would make enough for the two men plus the family when they got there. They would have to wait and pray for the men.

They left quickly, hugging the women one last time, before taking off.

The women didn't hear or see them for a week and were more than thankful to see them come through the door. Both men looked extremely tired but Louise immediately asked about the Taylors and what happened to them.

John began to explain that they reached the farm just as the light faded. "There was no light in the windows. First, we checked the porch and found the body of Ian's wife. Then we checked the bedroom, where we found Ian's lifeless body. He had died just before we got there because his body was still warm. The children were no where to be found. We checked the whole house and realized that one of the neighbors must have taken them."

James spoke up then and said, "We decided to make a work party and dig two graves in the back yard. That's what Ian wanted. The snow had drifted in the back yard, but we thought we could dig through it. We found out, when two neighbor women came while we were there, that Mrs. Bannister had the children, who were very sick, but she hoped they would survive. The women said they would call on some of the neighbor men to come and help and the women would gather and burn the sheets and bedding and clean the house of the foul smell and any contaminants. We made arrangements for two days hence. We placed Ian's body in a blanket on the porch as well, where it would keep cold until we came back to dig. Our hearts were heavy as we left to go to the farm. We knew we must all be careful because we don't know anything about this disease."

Louise was quiet until then when she said, "James you feel as I do that good food, good hygiene, fresh air and exercise is necessary in combating disease of any kind." Nodding he sat back while John continued.

"We went back to the farm to await and prepare. The men of the neighborhood came together to dig the graves and the women cleaned the house and burned the bedding. Sadness prevailed and I must say James out did himself, giving a great but brief sermon. I made two crosses for markers with their names on them and there were a lot of tears when they placed the markers on the graves."

"I pocketed the information Ian had left for me to follow up as soon as possible. In the meantime, a question arose about the children and that's when John spoke up," said James.

"I know that Meg would want to take care of the children, she had already indicated that desire, and I am in favor, but we will have to talk about it and where to look after them. They will need special care, I understand, to recover."

Mrs. Bannister was relieved saying, "That would be a great help, since I have other children to look after and I don't want them to get sick."

"We will work it out, thank you for taking them in now,"

"There was no other way, I could see Ian deteriorating fast and they were so hungry, poor mites," she answered tearing up again.

"Okay, I told her I would be in touch in the next day or so, with some idea of what to do, with James's help and guidance," John said.

"We watched the weather closely because we wanted to reach you as soon as possible. It had seemed to stay calm but there was

We came

no way that it would stay that way for long. As soon as we could ~~we came,~~" added James glancing at Louise.

There were a lot of tears when they finished explaining and Meg wanted to know more about the children.

"Mrs. Bannister and I spoke about the children and I reassured her we would take them as soon as possible. Am I right?" added John.

"Yes, but we will have to find a place to do just that," Meg spoke with deliberation but concern.

"There is a house, nearby that is empty right now. I believe the people just up and went back East, I can go and see about it," said John.

"By all means," replied Meg.

Louise spoke up then, "We will find all you need in the meantime. I can sew clothes for the children, and we will find beds and bed clothes, and anything else that you need."

James added to that, "We will pray that the poor mites, regain their health. I believe with good care and good food; they have a chance."

John was already out the door, before anyone could reply. They knew he was going to make sure it happened for they had all seen Meg's face light up and how quickly he reacted.

It didn't take long for the people to figure out what was needed. The house, needed some improvement, and a work party soon had it done. Louise was busy making curtains, securing bed clothes and she wanted to sew each child a new night dress. She had already ordered some flannelette and as soon as it came in, she got to work. By the end of the week all was ready for the children to be moved. That would be tricky business, but James was determined to see it done and done right, with as little fuss as possible. Bill and Liz got into the action as well, donating small much needed items. In the meantime, Meg was preparing herself as well. She contacted the doctor for instructions and he came as soon as he heard. He gave her all the information she needed and hoped that everything would work out. He also offered to come back more often, and would use the house as an office, when he did. That suited everyone. A doctor in town was what they wanted so badly.

Louise and Liz helped so that when the children arrived, Meg was ready for them. Between them all everything was wiped down and the doctor left strict orders for Meg to wear a mask and wash her hands often.

When she had settled each frail body into bed and made sure they were warm she couldn't help but call the women.

"A tiny face encircled by a mass of golden hair, smiled up at me and melted my heart. She cried and I found it hard not to cry with her. Ian was a little older, but small for his age, I thought, very thin and pale, with dark hair and lashes and ever so listless. He asked about his mother and father wondering where they were. I had to tell him but I also told him we would take them out to see the graves when they were stronger. He teared up but refused to cry and finally settled down. It was so sad!"

"It is sad and we are here to help you anytime," answered Liz.

"They are resting finally. Ian was restless so I sat beside him and rubbed his little back and soon he settled down. I told them I would get them some food and drink when they wake and I will bathe them before night," Meg continued as John came bursting in.

" How are you making out?"

"I am okay, but already I am going to have my hands full, but I love it, and my darling thank you for doing this for me,"

"Only for you, my dear," he said with a smile and pulled her aside for a hug.

"Wait, I must wash up, and make sure I don't contaminate you," she said sternly but with a smile.

"I may not be able to get in for some time, if the weather turns stormy. James and I will make out okay, but we have to look after the horses, and keep the fire going otherwise everything will freeze," John said with a glum look.

"I will worry about you, but don't worry about me, I will be very busy for the next while, working hard to bring these children to better health with the other women are all helping in one way or another. The next two months will tell, the doctor says, but with good care, he believes they will recover."

"Good, make sure you get your rest. I need you more than ever, and I can't wait until July," he winked and made to leave but not without giving her a kiss and hug that lasted a few minutes.

He had just left when Louise came sailing in.

"I finished the night clothes, see," and she showed Meg. A night dress for Mary and Ian. "I hope they like them,"

Meg laughed and said, "Let's show them to the children and they can try them on, that is if they are awake."

When they went into the bedroom, the children were indeed awake. They had heard the people talking and were waiting. And the ooh's and ah's indicated how excited the children were to receive something new. Little Mary couldn't help but prance around when she put the night dress on, but nearly keeled over.

She was still very weak. Ian put his on and was ever so pleased, saying, "It feels so nice and warm,"

"Good, it's my gift to you two," as Louise said as she hurried back to Liz's with a quick wave to Meg.

"What a nice thing to do, children. They will keep you nice and warm won't they?"

"Yes," came a dual answer. Both were going to climb back into bed, but Meg showed them the socks, she had knitted for them and they got excited all over again.

"Wow," said Ian, "It feels like Christmas, doesn't it Mary?"

"Oh, yeah," she smiled.

"Come put them on, and sit up. I will bring you some hot cocoa and a biscuit for your tea," Meg was in her glory, looking after these children and watching their little faces light up was such a treat she told Liz and Louise.

The weather turned very cold, again. No one ventured out very often for fear of frost bite. When the doctor made his call, he treated more with that than anything else. Stay indoors he kept saying, until the weather breaks. Meg reiterated how grateful she was for his visits, and he seemed pleased with the improvement on the children.

The cold kept all of them especially Meg constantly making sure the fires were kept going. She wore a warm stole at all times and made soup often. She had the help of neighbors as well.

Chapter Eight

Christmas

At last, at the beginning of December, the weather became less cold and although it snowed a lot, it was easier to get out and about. James and John made it in and picked up supplies. They didn't stay long, but made sure the women were okay before leaving. The wagons ~~were~~ changed to sleighs which were easier on the horses. *had been*

Soon it was the Christmas season. Everyone was busy making or baking for the festivities including Meg who worked with the children. Louise was a frequent visitor to see the children. She knew Meg was determined to make it a special Christmas this year, in spite of the weather and sickness, decorating the house with fir boughs that John brought her and paper chains made by the children to ~~put on~~ *decorate* them. The two women had ordered Christmas treats but didn't know if they would come in in time.

The days sped by, as the women worked on the festivities. Soon it was Christmas Eve. Louise and Meg were worried about the men. James had told Louise that he might not make it in Christmas eve, because he wanted to have a gathering of the neighbors to celebrate the birth of Christ. She knew that this would be a special time for him because he loved the church plays and music. She also wished that she could be a part of that but it was not to be so. She must be patient. Meg was also concerned but had not been brought up in the church. She would listen and learn.

Louise volunteered to visit Meg and tell the children the story of Jesus and when she did this some other families joined in to give Meg a lift for her diligent work. It turned out to be a wonderful evening. Everyone contributed something, whether it was food, words of wisdom or just plain friendliness. Louise and Meg were thrilled and couldn't wait to tell the men.

Christmas Day began bright and sunny during the morning. Louise was constantly looking out the window in hopes of seeing a sign of the horse and sled coming. She felt gloomy, until she heard the bells and realized they were on the horses driven by John and James. What a sight! She couldn't believe it and got so excited running out into the street waving and hollering, "Merry Christmas!"

It was a happy time all around. Even Meg and the children stood at the door and called to them. John jumped down at the door and picked Meg up like she was a rag doll and twirled her around to the children's delight.

James kept on going, but stopped to say hello to Louise before putting the horses in the barn calling, "Merry Christmas to all," He couldn't wait to hold Louise in his arms either. John came running after him to help and both men gathered up their packages and made for the houses as fast as they could.

James had a package for Louise and Louise in turn waited until they were seated to present hers. She had made James a new shirt in his favorite color. He could not believe it fit perfectly. "How did you do that?" he asked smiling. He already knew how clever she was from the ragged collars she remade by cutting off the bottom of his shirts to make new ones.

Louise motioned to Liz to come with her into the bedroom where she presented her with her wedding dress. Liz was ecstatic and danced around the room. Then she noticed another one and looking at Louise asked, "Is that one for Meg?" clapping her hands when Louise nodded.

"I also made a shirt for Bill," Louise added to which Liz was stunned.

"That is what you have been doing? Louise you are a wonder," and she hugged her and flew out to show Bill. Again, it fit beautifully and Bill asked her how in the world did she know his size.

"Oh, I have my ways," she answered.

"I can't show you, but Louise has made our wedding dresses and they are beautiful. I can't wait to wear mine and I can't wait to tell Meg."

"We will join Meg and John a while later. I also have gifts for the children," said Louise.

"What a wonderful surprise," said Bill who was still in disbelief. Both men refused to take the shirts off and paraded around the room to show their delight. When they finished parading, James came over to Louise and told her quietly he had made something for her but couldn't bring it, adding that it was a dresser with a mirror only for her. Louise clapped her hands and said," Oh, how I wanted one for so long, thank you my love," she beamed. Then he pulled her aside and presented her with a ring, that made her cry with happiness. It was her turn to waltz around showing it off. Then Liz joined the foray and showed one off as well. The women hugged one another in excitement.

Before they ate the simple dinner that Liz had prepared, James said a lovely grace including everyone and everything. After the meal of chicken, potatoes, peas, onion pie and sweets they sat back with a cup of tea and felt very special to be so blessed.

Before long, James indicated that they would have to leave, before it gets too dark. First they made their way over to Meg and John's, who had just finished their meal of the same. Of course, Liz had prepared enough for all.

Meg was smiling broadly, because she had received her engagement ring and was showing it off. John was also proudly showing off a pair of socks and slippers made by Meg. With all the excitement, two pairs of eyes excitedly watched because they too received socks and slippers and John had fashioned a toy horse out of wood and a doll that he commissioned Louise to make the clothes for. Louise had also sewed a shirt for John, a shirt for little Ian and a dress for Mary and produced it at this time. They were so excited and John was stunned and sat with his mouth open. He couldn't believe this woman.

Liz couldn't wait to tell Meg, what Louise had made for them, "Meg, Louise had made the most beautiful wedding dresses for us, you need to see them," at which Meg stood with her mouth open.

"It is my gift to both of you. You have been so wonderful to James and I and it is the one thing that I can do, besides cutting hair, that is," and they all laughed, for indeed she was in great need there.

"While you men are here, please look after the children for a short time, so Meg can go over and see the dresses, it won't take long," said Liz and before the men could answer, the women were off and running. Louise directed them to her bedroom where the dresses hung.

"Oh, my goodness!" cried Meg. "They are beautiful, so beautiful, I can't thank you enough, I made slippers for you Louise and Liz and socks for the men, but that is so little beside the dress.

"It is not small, I love what you have made for us," Louise said in earnest as they headed back to Meg's full of laughter and talk.

Spring

The weather stayed cold and blustery for the next two months, then within a day or so started to warm up. Snow was melting off the roof, leaving little rivulets running along the road. People were smiling as they slipped and slid through the puddles. It was a sign of spring.

Then a letter came for James Whiteley regarding the Taylors. When James got the letter, he informed the women that it said the children should be sent to relatives in Scotland. However, James thinking about it added, "I believe those children were born here, and will not have papers to travel abroad."

"They can't travel in the state they are in," Meg hastily replied, concerned about this letter and what it meant.

"Remember they are their only relatives," answered James. "We will have to wait and see. I will ask Louise to write and tell them the condition of the children. Say some prayers, ladies."

Meg worried about it. She was getting very fond of the children and could think of nothing else often talking to Louise about it. Both women wondered if they would be taken away. It would be so cruel. Meg discussed hiding them, but they both knew it wouldn't work. The children were improving but they were not ready for that much of a change. *of a new home or country*

The days went by, some cold and blowing, some crystal clear and beautiful, but forever changing. Then one day as the weather started to warm up, a pudgy, well dressed man, pushed his way into Meg's nursery, asking gruffly with a Scottish accent, "Who is in charge here?" Meg, surprised, answered, "I am, and just who are you?"

"I am a private investigator, sent by the Taylor family to locate two children belonging to Ian Taylor."

"What do you want with the children?" Meg asked studying him. She found him arrogant and was determined not to give him any information.

"I am instructed to take them back to Scotland to their family,"

"I see, even if the children are sick and confined to bed?"

"They can't be that sick," he replied, looking around the little house and noticing the sterile atmosphere.

"I assure you, they are sick, and if I may say so, you have no business being in here at all. This is a nursery and I do not appreciate anyone coming in from travelling, all dusty and unclean, without a doctor's permission." He backed off at that statement and decided to leave, but before he did he said, "I will be back, when the doctor arrives. I assure you Madam, that I will take these children back."

Meg was wild, so when he left, she checked on the children, who were asleep, slipped a coat on and ran to see Louise.

The man had already checked in with Liz, who gave him a room and offered some refreshment.

Louise saw him come in and wondered what he wanted.

When she saw, Meg, wild eyed and teary, she knew something was up. Meg, told her what he wanted and how arrogant he was. Louise immediately, said "I'll come over with you. We can't leave the children alone." When they got back to Meg's, the children were crying. Ian was calling for Meg who immediately went to him. He clung to her, saying, "I don't want to go to Scotland."

Meg answered him saying, "I don't want you to go either, and I will fight for you," and she meant it.

Louise quickly took in the situation and was alarmed, that someone would just come in and take children, just like that. She wanted to talk to James, before saying too much. The children were not able to travel right now. Surely, he would have to have a doctor's okay to do that. Poor little tykes! She nodded to Meg that she was leaving and went back to Liz's.

Liz was in a terrible mood when she got back. "I wish I had never set eyes on that man," she said with a vengeance. "He called this place a disaster and disgusting. I have never, ever, had someone so rude."

"I have a feeling about this man, Liz, I am wondering if he really is a detective, because they do not normally treat people like that. It seems to me that he is a dandy and maybe involved in the family business whatever that is, or maybe it has to do with money. We don't know very much about this family. I wonder if James has any information."

"I am sure, that unless he smartens up, I will have to ask him to leave."

"James and John should be coming in soon, the weather looks good, but there was still snow on the ground in places. Let's ask them."

A couple of days later, the men did come into town by horseback. When they arrived at Liz' and saw how upset the women were, they quickly took care of the horses and rushed back there.

Liz explained to them: We have this man staying here, that is rude and demanding and claims he is a detective from Scotland, looking for the Taylor children. I don't know where he went just now, but it might have been over to Meg's. He has been harassing her for the last two days, demanding to see the children and asking lots of questions. She has asked him to leave more than once.

John left immediately. James sat for a minute, drank some tea then uttered, "I need to meet with this man, at once. Louise, you look like you have something on your mind?"

"I question his credentials, James, because he is so demanding."

"Did you ask him for them?"

"He doesn't deal with women of such lower classes," she answered.

"Then we shall see, shall we?" He walked out and went over to Meg's, concerned that John might get very annoyed with him hanging around Meg.

He could hear John talking loudly, before he even knocked on the door. Meg answered and nodded to James to come in. Immediately, both men looked askance of the intruder, whereas he introduced himself as a detective from Scotland.

"How did you get here?" asked James.

"I managed to get to Saskatoon, and the bobby brought me out here to this hellish place. I can't believe that the Taylors lived here,"

"Mr. what is your name and where are your credentials?" asked James, as John looked on. "We are not going to release any information to you, until we see those and you can stop being demanding and rude as well."

"These people have immigrated from your own country and are not the lower class, as you put it," said John.

Meg heard the children who were quietly listening to the conversation until James came in, then started whispering. She went into the bedroom and stayed there. She was very unhappy with this man and his slicked hair and pointy beard, smelling like perfume.

James realized that this man had alienated all these people in a very short time and that didn't fit a detective's description at all. So he pressed the issue of credentials until at last Mr. Detective produced a hand written letter.

"This is not a credential. I think you are here under false pretenses and should leave immediately, before I call the Redcoats to investigate."

"Okay, okay, I am related to Ian Taylor by marriage. His mother asked if I would investigate and find the children and bring them back to Scotland."

"I am afraid that that is impossible, you see, Ian and his wife died of tuberculosis, and the children have shown signs of the same, so they are in isolation here to be treated. They are also Canadian born, so they do not have papers to go abroad. The farm is up for sale, with the money going toward the children's care. Meg has been nursing them since they lost their parents and doing an excellent job and under a doctor's care as well. Now for all your blustering, you could have just explained why you came to the women and they would have understood. You owe them an apology. If you don't like the accommodation, perhaps you would like to spend a few nights at their farm house and learn a few things."

"That would be a good idea, I would like to do that, if you would show me how to get there," he said a little subdued, but still not revealing his real name.

"We can arrange that tomorrow. Be ready early! And remember an apology or she will boot you out, and you will have to sleep in the horse barn with the mice."

"Okay, okay, I will. I will also be ready in the morning,"

James winked at John, who caught on and kept a straight face, but found it difficult.

"Good idea, James. I will be ready as well."

"I am going to make sure he apologizes before night. We need to find out his real name. I don't believe he is telling the whole truth and his disregard for women worries me," said James as the two men left.

He did apologize to the women. They accepted but Liz told him she would not tolerate any more disruption or posturing from him at all.

Early next morning, John and James rode up to the entrance with an extra horse for this man. When he saw the extra horse, he exclaimed that he did not know how to ride, and couldn't they have taken a carriage? James explained that they did not have a carriage and in the spring when snow was still on the ground the best way to get around was by sled or horseback. After hearing that, he did his best to get on the horse, but it took several attempts. John, couldn't help but laugh and the women had the good sense to remain out of sight but laughed wholeheartedly.

A couple of days later, John returned and told the women what happened on that little trip they took. "It took a while before he got used to the horse and only then were they able to pick up the pace. After some time, we stopped for a break and got down off our horses. We opened our flask of tea, but the so-called detective had another flask which we realized was not tea and that in itself worried James. When we came in sight of the Taylor house, he cried out, "This cannot be their place, surely. It looks so dilapidated and bleak."

I couldn't help but answer him, "What did you expect, some kind of mansion?"

"I can't stay here. It's impossible. I must go back," he said.

"To where?" I asked.

"To Mrs. Long's, at least that place looked lived in."

I looked at James who spoke up then. "This is where Ian and his wife lived until they passed. We were going to leave you here for the night. You wanted to see where they lived. You can ride back yourself. We have our own homes out here, so we will not accompany you.

Where upon the detective immediately turned his horse around and left, without even a thank you, good bye or anything.

"Meg will be worried about the children, I told James. Perhaps I should ride in as well and allay her fears."

"Good idea, he might get lost, especially if he keeps nipping at that flask he has. He may be drunk by the time he gets back, and grumpy," replied James, *who tells this story*

"On the way into town, I couldn't help laugh. The so-called detective nearly fell off his horse several times and was stopping often, probably trying to figure out if he was on the right track. You probably heard what happened when we got back. He was in a rare mood, laughing and going on about women. I was getting worried, because I knew that Liz would not tolerate a drunk in the house. At the house, he fell off his horse, but got up and just left the horse standing there. I yelled at him to look after his horse."

"Oh you can do that," he called back laughing.

"Then he rushed to the door, banging on it and calling, Let me in! I yelled at him to 'just open the door, you fool and went on to the barn. I knew a problem would arise. Just as I got back to the house, I heard an angry voice asking him who did he think he was, some high mucky muck and you can leave right now or you can smarten up and go to bed. I guess Louise you heard the commotion and came out just as Liz was telling him off. Bless you, for asking him what his real name was. I waited to hear that."

Louise piped up then saying, "he called himself, 'Donovan' and added that he expected breakfast at 7:00 am then I will be leaving this dammed place."

"Well you must have heard the rest. I heard you say he almost fell into his door, but managed to stay upright until he slammed it shut and it sounded like he fell again. I imagine you decided to leave it alone, and pray he would sleep it off in the night," said John.

The women told John that Mr. Donovan left the next morning and they were more than thankful. They really didn't care how, when or where he went, as long as he did for he was extremely rude.

Spring Planting

The days got warmer and warmer and people were getting ready for spring cleaning and farmers were getting ready for sowing. James came in more often now and was planning his own crop and buying the necessary supplies. He never forgot to chat with Louise though and always hugged her in plain sight, which in itself was a change. Louise who was now kept busy cutting hair and sewing when the light was good, often feeling there wasn't enough time in the day. There was always something to do she told James, so he wouldn't worry about her. He seemed satisfied, but told her he couldn't wait until July.

He also told her that the Railroad was coming through and that the store at Wirral was moving to their town which was going to be called Lashburn, after a Railroad Solicitor named Lash and burn which means a Scottish creek. It means you can count on more people and business coming. They are moving the school

1406 here as well but it needs upgrading. Sounds like God is answering our prayers.

There was an urgency in the air for the next few months as supplies and people came. The Mounties or Redcoats as Louise called them, came often checking on the immigrants and supplying tents and information. They were kept busy, as were the local men building as the lumber supply came. It was becoming more and more like a town and Liz was excited but having trouble keeping up to the traffic. The women worked from dawn to dusk, including Meg who was busy with the children. She was enjoying the teaching aspect and explained to them that if the time came that their relations found a way to take them back to Scotland, they were to use it as a tool to educate themselves and learn as much as possible about their ancestry, and when they were ready they could make their own decision to come back and she would welcome them wholeheartedly. That seemed to satisfy Ian, but Mary questioned it frequently. Meg told her she had to be brave and her brother would be her advocate.

Louise, Meg and Liz were getting excited, for their wedding day was fast approaching. No one had heard from Rev. Lloyd, but Louise was sure he would come

Chapter Nine

Weddings

Time was flying by as the women, readied themselves for the upcoming nuptials. The excitement of a government official coming stirred up a frenzy of activity in town. People were coming *arriving* in and setting up shop wherever they could find a place. Supplies and goods were coming in steady.

Louise, Meg and Liz seemed oblivious to the hustle and bustle as they sewed and cleaned with such compulsion and exuberance that inspired all the rest to do the same. They constantly checked the weather as the days went by. The men didn't come in as often, but were aware of the changes in town.

July 1st was fast approaching. The house had been decorated for the occasion, the menu was decided on and the necessary supplies ordered. Louise and Liz handled the cafe and rooms, while Meg concentrated on the children. She taught them their numbers, alphabet and reading and writing, following instructions sent to her. Besides, she took them on short field trips, learning the names of grasses and flowers, and birds and animals of the prairie. They were so interested in everything. She professed to Louise that teaching them was easy.

The weather was warm when the day approached and looked like it was going to be perfect. The only thing missing was the minister and no one had heard from him, but Louise was always optimistic.

"He will come, I know it. We must believe and pray."

The first of July dawned sunny, with not a cloud in the blue, blue sky. The women laughed and joked as they prepared themselves for the day. The cafe was closed as were the rooms. When the men appeared, oohs and ahs sounded everywhere. What a sight they were in their dark suits, white shirts and ties, and shoes that shone.

All was ready, but no minister, until early afternoon. That's when a carriage pulled up in front of the house bearing a tall man with a bowler hat. He looked like a well-dressed government man and people remained aloof at first. No one knew him, until he spoke. That's when Louise spoke up. She remembered his voice from Halifax. It was Rev. Lloyd and when they learned that, they clapped and cheered as he made his way toward them. He greeted them all wholeheartedly as they stood there in complete silence, hanging on to his every word.

"I am honored to perform a marriage today, and maybe more than one. Then I would like to talk to the people here to find out what I can do to help." Someone spoke up then, saying," We want to build a church, we already have a school,"

"Great, we will talk about that," he answered, then smiling he asked for James Whiteley and Louise Hemsley. That is my first promise."

"If you don't mind there are another two couple wishing to marry today as well, a Margaret Ward and John Wiley; Elizabeth Long and Bill Lance," said James as he introduced himself.

Then Bill suggested that they go into the house for the ceremony. He promised the people watching outside that they would see the bride and groom later. He also announced that there would be fun and games going on during the day and everyone could take part. After all, he said this is the day Saskatchewan becomes part of Canada. There will be speeches too, on a platform that had been made for that purpose. He did not know who the official was but he would be a government man. When he looked around, he was surprised to see so many people with more coming all the time.

Inside the house, three women were dressed in their wedding outfits, so when James, Rev. Lloyd, Bill and John along with Mary and Ian came in, there was oohs and ahs again.

"You look bootiful, Mama Meg, just bootiful," said Mary which created a lot of laughter.

"Thank you my darling child," replied Meg.

"You all look fantastic," said Ian. It was a word he had just learned.

Rev. Lloyd took charge then and assembled Louise and James at the front. Some of the close neighbors came in then to join the gathering and fell in behind the couple. Meg and John stood up for James and Louise and they would in turn stood up for them and Bill and Liz. When the Reverend finished with James and Louise, there was a lot of clapping, but he hushed them and proceeded to marry the next couple and so on. Then he spoke on the Grace of God and the importance of prayer and blessed everyone.

The day was indeed a lively affair. However, James and Louise, remained separate and decided to have a quick chat with the minister and start for home and their new life. Meg and John joined the children in the games, but only after Meg had changed. Liz and Bill were back in the kitchen hard at work as well. They would all take a much needed rest at the end of the celebrations. Today the town was alive and it was wonderful to see. It would be one to remember for the rest of their lives.

James and Louise heard later that you could hear the excitement in the street. An elderly man brought out his fiddle and a couple of others joined him with an accordion and a guitar and the people responded by dancing in the street. It was a gala affair. The day ended with fireworks. Some had already gone home, after having tasted all the goodies that were offered around town, but others remained for the fireworks, something they hadn't ever seen. Everyone claimed it was the beginning of a bustling new town with hundreds of possibilities.

James and Louise went home, quiet but happy after longing for this day for so long.

"I wish my father could have been here, and Jimmy, for he idolized you," said Louise who couldn't help but smile in spite of the fact that she missed them.

"We shall send them a letter informing them of our wedding and what a day it has been," James said, and added, "I am the happiest man on God's earth now I am sure, thank you, my Louise."

Louise was in a whirl, thinking about the day. When they arrived home she noticed the new bed, cupboards, a new big stove and above all a wooden floor. She danced around the house singing James praises and he just watched her and laughed. Then he grabbed her and held her in his arms for a very long time, until she kissed his cheek. He looked at her again and kissed her full on the lips, awakening so much inner emotion.

"We have nothing to do tonight, but to enjoy one another," he said as he motioned toward the new bed, which was decked out in a new mattress, linen and a fine quilt.

He explained that the quilt was a gift from Liz and Bill and the linen from some of the neighbors. Just as they were preparing for bed, they heard a deafening noise.

"What in the world?" cried Louise just as the door burst open and a group of neighbors came bouncing in. shouting, "Surprise."

"This is a chivaree, something we do out here. We have brought goodies to eat and gifts for you. They crowded around wishing and hugging. It was midnight before they had tea and cakes and opened the gifts, *or departed* Louise was so tired by this time; she could barely keep her eyes open. She looked askance at James, who winked and nodded, tired as well. Both fell into bed and were sound asleep before either could say goodnight. When they woke, the sun was shining in the window, and all was calm. James, rolled over and taking Louise in his arms, said happily, "Good morning, Mrs. Whiteley, my love," and she answered with a kiss. They spent most of the morning in bed, where they sealed their marriage vows forever. Both in a state of euphoria.

"What an end to a blessed day," exclaimed Louise, as she hugged her husband one more time before getting up.

The next day was clean-up in town. Liz and Bill were exhausted but the reverend was still there and he wanted to talk to them. He had spoken to James and promised him help in building a church. He was so enthusiastic about it that he inspired people everywhere. He joined in the clean-up and talked to the children as well as their parents. He wanted to know them all. He had that type of face that wasn't what you would call handsome but a voice that made you sit up and take notice. They would remember him.

He was to leave the next day, but delayed it because he wanted to visit James and Louise before he left in order to hear his theory on a building and location and more. He commissioned a buggy and driver to take him to their place. Liz questioned him about it, but he put her at ease telling her it had been preplanned. He wanted to enjoy the countryside at the same time, looking off into the distance.

He surprised James and Louise when he drove in their yard. They definitely were not expecting company especially after the honeymoon surprise. They welcomed him anyway and Louise set about making tea, while James and the reverend conversed.

"I feel that perhaps it would be a good thing to ask the government for help with the school. I understand it needs upgrading and a teacher. The school could be used as a church on Sunday, until we can get support for a church," the reverend said.

"Perhaps, you are right. A school is a necessity if we are to grow at all," answered James.

They agreed on a lot of principles and ideals and through it all, James and Louise knew they could count on the reverend. It ended in a prayer, which was led by James thanking God for the reverend and for the last few days. He added that many people were looking forward to developing this area. Rev. Lloyd left with a promise to come back.

They enjoyed the next few weeks with each other. Then late one afternoon, James called Louise to look at the sky for a storm was looming. When she did, she was fascinated yet apprehensive. It was very dark and looked ominous.

"What does it mean, strong wind, lots of rain?" she asked.

"I know you witnessed a storm when you came. This time you are going to be truly tested," James answered with a concerned look on his face. It was apparent that Louise had no idea what a huge storm meant to the farmers in the area.

"I'm going to need to see to the horses and make sure there's nothing that will fly around and do damage," he spoke as he put on his coat.

Louise watched the storm as it came closer. She did not really know what to do. She had brought her clothes off the line and her water pail was indoors. She remained at the open door.

Suddenly the wind started to pick up. Thunder and lightning was a way off yet, but she could see and hear it. There had been genuine concern on James face, but she kept quiet and, waited. When she heard the first thunder crash overhead, she jumped. James had told her to keep the door closed so she did and sat in silence as the lightning flashed and thunder roared overhead, and the rain poured as she waited for James to come back. He was gone quite awhile before she saw him, drenched, running for the house. Just as he made the door, the first hail stones bounced off the door step.

"I daresay, we could lose our crop this year, if this keeps up," he said taking off his coat and hat. He no sooner got his boots off when the door burst open and John ran in saying, "Sorry, but I am soaked to the skin. I was going in to see Meg, but the rain came down so hard, I couldn't even see. I put my horse in your shed, James. I sure hope you don't mind. I don't like this storm at all," gasping for breath as Louise motioned for him to take off his coat and boots and sit by the stove.

"Not a problem, John. I am glad you stopped, get dried off and we'll have some tea if Louise can pull her way from the window."

Louise, laughed, "I have never witnessed such a storm. Oh, my look at the size of those hail stones?" At that the men moved quickly to glance over her shoulder. A few groans almost drowned out the thunder which was preceded by a flash of lightning that lit up the whole sky.

They sat down depressed, listening to the drone of rain and hail. Then suddenly it became quiet and when they looked out a rainbow appeared in the sky, but the yard was white with hailstones. By the time they had their tea and biscuits, it was twilight. The hail had almost melted and formed puddles of water around the yard.

"Perhaps, you should stay with us tonight and leave in the morning. I can pitch some hay in for your horse and water them if you like. Were you working on your house?" James asked.

"Yes, I guess in a way. I have been scouting the ponds west of here. I heard that beavers had been cutting down trees around streams and thought I could make use of those and it wouldn't cost anything either and they should be dry already," John answered.

"Good plan, did you find any?"

"Yes, quite a lot and I am going out with a wagon as soon as possible. Right now though, if you don't mind, the road will be flooded in places, so it would be better travelling in the day time. Meg will worry, I know, but will understand I am sure."

"I will make up a bed for you. You can wear one of James robes and I will hang your clothes to dry during the night," said Louise.

After checking on the horses, both men left their clothes out for Louise to hang up to dry and crawled into bed. Louise busied herself hanging the clothes and stoking the fire, before she got ready for bed herself. She could hear John snoring already. *The sooner Meg comes out the better.*

Next morning, after surveying the damage, the men were satisfied that the hail had not done much damage and everything settled down. Harvesting was soon the topic of discussion.

Fall

Time flew by and soon it was fall. The air was heavy with ripening vegetation and the leaves were changing color and littering the roadways. Everyone was rushing to get finished before the snow fell. It would be easier this year, since James and Louise could cuddle up in bed together. It was different for their friends as well.

Meg continued to teach the children and John was working hard at getting their home ready for them. He couldn't wait until they could settle there. Liz and Bill were kept busy with new people coming all the time.

Fall was always a very busy time on the farms. The women were kept busy feeding their men and sometimes others. But as *usual, the fall*

all falls, ~~they~~ never lasted long enough it seemed. The demand for rooms was slowing as well, so Liz and Bill were getting a breather. Meg kept working with the children but was getting excited at moving to the farm. She reported the children were progressing at a good pace. Still concerned about their move to Scotland *she was* preparing them for that time. However, she also realized she needed to focus on John.

Nothing seemed to happen in the next two months as harvest time came to a stop and winterizing began in full swing. Then a letter came for James. Bill rode out to the farm with it, thinking it might be important. They were surprised to see him but <u>also</u> pleased. James thanked him for making the effort, but <u>also</u> for the opportunity to visit as well.

Louise was curious about the letter, and advised James to open it. He did so and sat quietly for some time before answering their anxious glances.

"It's from Scotland, from Ian's relatives. They have been in touch with the doctor *who* ~~that~~ is treating the children and find that they are recuperating ~~and doing~~ very well. In the spring they will be sending a child minder to collect the children and take them back. Originally they had suggested January, but the Doctor advised them that it was not a good time to send anyone to this country in the middle of winter."

"You will have to tell Meg. I know that she will be heart broken, but there was naught that could be done," added Louise.

"I will tell her if you like, when I return. You are right, she will be heart broken, but I do believe that she also understands only too well," said Bill taking a second piece of cake. "Maybe I should have another cup of tea before I start back," he said as he winked at Louise. He was enjoying the visit.

"Come out again, Bill and bring Liz next time. She really needs a break,"

"Absolutely, by the way Jim/James, did Rev. Lloyd have any thoughts on the church we been talking about?" asked Bill.

"Yes, he did and I have sent a letter to the government in Ottawa, regarding the school house from Wirral that needs to be expanded. Rev. Lloyd suggested we might use the school as a church until we get help from them."

"Oh, sounds like a plan," answered Bill

"I want to start on the building in the spring if possible, and the neighbors are all in accord," said James.

Bill headed back to the rooming house and Liz after telling them that he was a very happy man at this time in his life.

Thanksgiving

Soon a plot had been decided for the church and the school addition started with everyone pitching in. Both James and Louise were excited about the school house and how everyone had responded.

John too joined in the excitement. He so wanted his little family to be settled on the farm by winter and by the looks, it was going to happen.

Meg was excited at ~~going~~ _moving_ to the farm, but also a bit apprehensive knowing that she had no control over the children leaving in the spring. She maintained though, that she would make this Christmas the best ever for the children, one they would never forget. She loved those children like they were her very own. John feared that this day would come, but he would help Meg reconcile to the idea that one day she would see them again, even if it meant selling the farm to make enough money to travel back to Scotland. He would find a way.

Right now, Meg was busy planning a Thanksgiving meal for the children and her man. She loved him dearly and wanted only the best. As soon as he said move, she would be ready and the children were looking forward to going as well. They were making posters for thanksgiving to hang around the house, for all to see. They were very creative and Meg was so proud of them. Even little Mary was joining in whole heartedly. She was the artistic one, and gave Ian pointers along the way. It was a joy to watch them interact. Meg wanted to show Louise, James, Bill, Liz and especially John just what they had done. She wanted to make a meal for them all. They ~~have~~ _had_ been so reliant, thoughtful and friendly throughout.

She was pondering all this when she heard a knock on the door, followed by a greeting from Louise. Excited she jumped up and hugged her. They were both glad to see each other.

"We came in for supplies today, but I wanted to know when Dr. Taylor is coming next?" Louise asked.

Meg looked at Louise, saying, "Is something wrong?"

"No, I just need to ask him some questions,"

"Louise, what are you saying?" Then as if a light bulb went on, Meg shouted, "Oh, Louise, you are with child,"

"I had thought so, but I know I am not at the moment. I need to ask some questions."

"Okay, I won't say anything, but don't be alarmed if Liz asks. That woman is very astute, believe me, I know," replied Meg.

They sat down to tea, just as Liz dropped in. She joined them at the table, saying," I was hoping to ask Louise something. She looks a little pale, and I was wondering if she was with child."

Meg started to laugh. "Liz, I was wondering the same thing. Unfortunately, Louise is not."

"Okay, but I know you are not feeling good. If you need anything, Louise, just ask me," said Liz, pouring herself a cup of tea. They sat there talking pleasantly for almost an hour, when, Liz rose and got ready to leave. She smiled at the other two and put her fingers to her mouth saying, "Maybe soon."

Both women ended up laughing for the next few minutes. Just as they were washing up the cups, James came in to say he was ready to go.

"Come and have a cup of tea, first," asked Meg.

"We've had a great chat, but I want you both to come in for Thanksgiving, it will be my treat this year. You both have done so much for me and I want to give back a little of that good will."

"Of course, we will. Can I bring anything?" Louise asked adding "perhaps some bread loaves?"

"Oh, Louise, of course, that would be lovely," answered Meg.

All the while, James just smiled at the two women. He saw how happy they were chatting with one another. It was good for Louise and he decided then and there, they needed to do this more often for her sake. It became quite evident now to James, how lonely it was for Louise especially when he was at work or out and about.

Thanksgiving came and went, leaving Louise in a blur. She was not feeling that great. James was endearing at those times. He made the tea and kept things going. He was concerned however, that she didn't feel like eating. He was going to make sure she saw Dr. Taylor the next time he was in town. Winter was upon them and he worried about the roads getting blocked and decided that perhaps Louise would be better to stay in town.

When he broached the plan to her, she was not impressed and refused to go. She agreed that perhaps if she was in the family way, she might need to be close to a doctor, but right now she said she was just fine and that settled it. James smiled to himself. She could be feisty.

The snow did indeed come, blocking roads and walkways, making feeding animals more difficult. However, these men were now accustomed to harsh winters and worked with a very positive attitude. James was more concerned about Louise.

Christmas was coming up fast, and as soon as possible, they would change the wagon over to skis, to make it easier driving. James offered room for John's supplies because he did not have skis for his wagon which had been fixed alright but was not as sturdy as it should be. John was grateful for the help and was planning on bringing the family out at Christmas if the weather cooperated. It was all he could think about.

Louise gradually felt a little better, but still did not have an appetite and worried about it. She was anxious to see the doctor again and approached James about it. He was also concerned and suggested they would make the trip into town as soon as possible.

Within the week, James decided that they should get into town, before the weather turned cold and windy, because Louise was beginning to look extremely tired. She needed to see the Doctor. It would take a load off his mind if she would stay with Liz until the doctor came and if all was well he would go and get her. When he approached Louise, she immediately agreed.

The next day, the sun came out and was so bright that when you looked at the snow, it almost blinded you. They made it into town without too much trouble and immediately Louise went to see Meg, to find out about the doctor. He was due in a couple of days, so that calmed her. She would indeed stay with Liz for a few days, then she wanted to go back to the farm. As soon as people found out she was there, she was in demand for hair cuts.

Liz was not the least surprised. Louise was good at what she did and the people liked her. However, right now, she had to take it a little easier and Liz demanded she do that. Liz was concerned about her, especially after James mentioned that she was not feeling well and losing weight.

When Louise saw the doctor, he prescribed some medication for her. He told her she was as fit as any woman. She was in the first stages of being with child and still had a while to go but he wanted to keep an eye on her. He would make extra visits to accommodate that. Louise was happy to hear that and she willingly accepted all his suggestions. This baby was very precious and she wanted to be careful. She could plan her days closer to the time. Her sewing would have to take a Sabbath as well as hair cutting. Perhaps, they should request a hair dresser from Saskatoon to come once a month or maybe stay. Sewing wasn't good in the winter with the short days and coal-oil lamps. *She could do some hand work though.* Liz met her at the door and quizzed her, genuinely worried.

James came in about the same time, and of course wanted to talk to Louise. She smiled at him saying, "I am as healthy as a horse; so don't you worry. This baby will be delivered sometime in late August. The last months, the doctor requested I stay in town and I agreed. So you will have to put up with me until then. He also said my morning sickness should subside soon, if I behave."

That started them all laughing. James however, was not quite satisfied with what Louise said. He left to go to the stables, but stopped by Meg's on his way to talk to the doctor. He learned that she needed to take some medication which the doctor would send out and had to take it easy for the next while. That satisfied him. He thought Louise was being a bit too positive. He would make sure that she took it easier. Now that winter was upon them, there would be more time for reading and chatting.

Time went on, and the weather continued to get colder and snowier until everything was covered with a quilt of white. Louise looked out the small window in wonder at the vastness of the land. It was at one of these moments that she missed her home back in England where buildings and people were always around. It was so quiet here, she felt like she was in a total wilderness. James sensed her anxiety now, and made an excuse that they had better go to town to get some supplies before the roads got too difficult to travel. He wondered too maybe she should see the doctor again. She could stay at Liz's until he came. It was something he did not want to do, but for her sake, he decided it was for the best. She still had some time to go.

Plans were made to go in the next day, so for the moment, Louise seemed to settle down to tat. Her hands were busy most of the time, between cooking, mending and handicrafts. He was amazed at the dexterity of her hands. Her work was so dainty and perfect. Her cleverness in determining someone's size simply stunned them all. No wonder people were forever looking for her to do some sewing. However, for now she had to slow down and Liz and Meg were the only ones he knew that could convince her to do so. He could only hope and pray. He looked forward to having a child around. He thought about her brother, Jimmy, who at the time seemed to be a nuisance but he would welcome that nuisance now.

They made ready for the trip into town. James made sure there was ample hay in the sleigh to shield them from the cold. He had put on his long underwear when he arose, although sometimes it itched, but it would keep him warm. The horses were needing exercise and ready to trot. Louise sneezed several times before getting seated. She laughed as she held her hand to her mouth. "I think that the hay is causing me to sneeze," sneezing again.

" We'll get going and maybe fresh air will help," said James, hoping against hope that it would, otherwise it was going to be a long ride.

Off they went and finally Louise settled down and the sneezing stopped, at least momentarily. It was cold but there was very little wind, so the drive was enjoyable. Louise was so looking forward to seeing the girls and chatting with them realizing how she missed their companionship.

They arrived in town by noon, and while James stabled the horses, Louise stopped in to chat with Meg. Dr. Taylor was there and welcomed her to come and talk to him. She told him what was happening and he listened carefully. Then after examining her, he said, "I believe that everything is okay. But I must insist again that you rest often," at which Louise raised her eyebrows in question.

"You mean I am going to be sick the whole time and what about my loosing weight?"

"I will prescribe some more medicine for you, that should help your appetite, but I emphasize the fact that you take it easy. I happen to know a little about farm life and how much you ladies do," as he watched her with concern.

"I am planning on coming into town for the last two months, or rather my husband is planning on it," she spoke with firmness but not convincingly.

"I would like to speak with your husband, if I may?" he asked.

"Of course, he would like that," she answered.

At that moment James came into the house and nodded hello to Meg and the doctor. He looked at Louise questioningly. "The doctor wants to talk to you," she answered him anticipating his next question.

"Alright," he said and both went into the bedroom that he called his appointment room, while Meg and Louise, sat in the kitchen, talking to the children, who were all ears at this time. Meg couldn't help but notice how interested they were in all this. She motioned to Louise, about big ears around, to which Louise nodded. They engaged the children in small talk, asking about what they were learning etc. They told Louise that they were getting ready to move to the farm and by the look on their faces, they were extremely excited.

James came out of the bedroom, with Dr. Taylor behind. They both smiled at the children talking so animatedly about moving.

"Did John say when you were moving?" asked the doctor, " I don't know what I will do without you all," he said motioning with his hands.

"No, problem, doctor, I will be here when you come in," said Meg quickly. She was going to miss all this too, but on the other hand, there would be other things that would have to be done.

"We will be moving in the spring," she added realizing that she hadn't answered his question.

Chapter Ten

As the weeks went by and winter closed in on Louise and James, both tried to busy themselves, but the daylight hours were so short that Louise got bogged down on some of her projects. James, however, seemed to be calm and collected and kept his hands busy with his latest project. When Louise finally took a good look at what he was doing, she realized that he was crafting a cradle.

"Oh, my, James, that is going to be beautiful," she said happily.

"I was hoping so," he answered, stopping only to look up at her smiling.

"I know that I am going to move into town at some time but I still have some time to go. I would like to talk to the women again."

"The road is open so far, as long as we don't get a wind storm," he said shrugging. Then adding, "We will cross that bridge when we get there," leaning over and hugging her. He knew she was anxious about the baby but he would not let anything happen, if he could help it. He prayed for assistance every morning and night.

"We will meet with the neighbors, tomorrow night. I will alert them to our predicament should something happen. We will have our prayer meeting and discuss the new church and what we will do for Christmas. I would like a pageant." He smiled to himself, when he thought about the piano he had ordered, but now, he needed to distract Louise. He knew she was worrying.

"Oh, good, I need to talk to the women about certain things, after all they all have had babies and they are doing well," she stated matter of fact.

James just nodded in agreement, carrying on sanding and fitting a board.

Louise, busied herself, readjusting the curtains, and cleaning whatever she could. The place was as neat as a pin, but she continued to straighten, dust or adjust wherever. It was routine with her, after long years of caring for her father and brother, while her mother sewed. She sighed as she thought of those days when she was so tired, that often she would take time on the way home after delivering a parcel, to sit and rest and daydream. It seemed so far away and long ago.

Christmas was coming up fast, and Louise was at a loss at to what to do about sewing, the light was so poor and she wanted to order more material but hadn't had the opportunity to do so. She wanted to go to town.

"After this week end, can we try and get to town? I need to order some more material and thread and a few other things," she said looking askance at James.

"Of course, lets try for Monday, unless of course it is snowing and blowing. But we will try, yes we will try," he answered firmly.

That put her mind at ease for the moment. He noted she was quite moody lately and he suspected it was due largely to being isolated. It hadn't dawned on him that it might have a lot to do with her anxiety on being with child.

Sunday morning was bright and sunny. Louise was elated. She was so anxious to talk to the other women. This day was going to be glorious, she thought as she plodded around the room making breakfast. James liked his porridge, but she really didn't, although she did try to appease him.

Louise dressed with care and was ready long before James came with the horses. He noted that she was anxious to get going, so he tried to be quick. Soon they were off. The horses were ready for a run and showed it. It didn't take long to get to the neighbors, where they were welcomed enthusiastically. Louise joined the women in the house, while James secured the horse and sleigh.

They chatted happily, telling Louise all about birthing and the pros and cons of staying out on the farm too long. A snowstorm could be a problem. Louise was finding it hard to absorb all that was being said, but she remained calm, until James came in with the other men.

Immediately James called for a prayer and began a service, like Louise had never witnessed. They sang hymns, said prayers, talked about sins and about blessings. The latter, being the last topic and the best. He acknowledged that they were to become parents and that both were ecstatic. It was just the inspiration that Louise needed. She couldn't wait to tell James just that. After a luncheon, they left for home before it got dark.

"I am so proud of you, James. That was the inspiration that the people here need so desperately," Louise said with enthusiasm.

"I am glad that you liked it, for I meant every word," he said calmly adding, "Tomorrow we will go to town and you can make your purchase or order whatever and I shall do the same."

He would be checking on the piano that he had ordered and some of the other things he needed. The rest of the way home went in silence as each were deep in thought. Tonight, they would retire early, so that they could get an early start in the morning.

Morning wasn't exactly what they anticipated. It was snowing and blowing, so much so you could not see very far. The roar of the wind, made Louise shiver. There was no way they were going anywhere. Hopefully the wind will die down by nightfall. Louise was extremely disappointed and sat looking out the window willing it to calm.

"These are the kind of storms, that we can get in the winter. That is why it is important to be prepared having enough food, water and shelter for both human and animals. I believe this is the first winter storm for you, Louise," he said with concern in his voice.

He had been through a number of storms and had always made out okay. However, he knew some who hadn't fared so well, but he wasn't going to say anything for fear of disturbing Louise and that he could not stand.

"We will plan to go as soon as it lets up," hugging her as he spoke.

"Not a problem, I am just disappointed, I guess, but I will get over it," she answered, clinging to him.

The storm raged all day and most of the night, but when they awoke the next morning, everything was calm. Snow drifts appeared everywhere. Louise thought it looked beautiful. The sun was coming up and shadows were appearing everywhere.

"What a change!" she said with fervor.

"We will wait until, midday, then I will try to get our sleigh uncovered and the horses hooked up," sounding not too enthusiastic and commenting further that the drifts could be a problem.

James eventually went out all bundled up as Louise would say. He came back though and decided that to go to town then would not be a good thing. He explained to Louise that the sky looked ominous and that they should wait. He was sure another storm was brewing. Louise sat down disappointed, but took up her needles and starting knitting. He noticed that she did not look up for some time and that was unlike her. Could she be worrying about something else, he wondered.

"Louise, I do not want to take chances travelling in this weather," smiling and giving her a hug.

She sighed and answered, "I know, I'm just with child."

"Make us some tea, and we will sit and chat for a while. You know, I Love you, and want what's best for both of us," to which she only nodded.

Two days later, they made it into town, and luckily Dr. Taylor was there, so Louise was pleased. First she chatted with the doctor then went to the general store for supplies. Only then did she stop and talk to the women at Liz's. They noticed a change in Louise and decided that it was the largely because of what Meg had gone through previously. It was Meg who brought it out in the open.

"Louise, are you worried because of what I went through?" she asked.

"It could be, I am just anxious, I guess. I'm afraid of getting stuck out in the country and having James deal with me," shaking her head.

" You still have some time but you are coming into town for the last two months, aren't you?"

"Yes, but I don't know if that will be soon enough. I could be out in the timing,"

"Dr. Taylor said you are very close in the timing, so quit worrying," added Liz.

"You are right, I'm just with child. Let's talk of something else," Louise said as she sat down to drink her tea.

Just then James and Bill came in, both taking off their coats and boots, before sitting down at the table. James looked at the women, and noticed everything went quiet when they came through the door.

"Okay, what's up?" he asked, looking directly at Louise.

"We were analyzing Louise' anxiety, if you must know. I do believe we have resolved the issue. She can fill you in later," replied Liz.

James and Bill laughed and started talking about Christmas and the pageant James was planning.

"Pageant?" the women spoke in unison.

"Yes, pageant. It is something that you women could get involved in planning. I have the Christmas story somewhere in my belongings. It should not be hard to do. We have the children and Louise is good at making costumes, if we can find enough material and I am sure that we can." answered James.

The women looked at one another, and Louise spoke first, "Why that is a wonderful idea. It will take some planning, but I believe we are up to it. We can ask Meg and the children to join us. They would be excited, I am sure,"

"Great idea. James," said Bill, adding, "And if you need something built, I can do that,"

With that, James nodded to Louise that they must be going. As they were getting ready to leave, a redcoat as Louise still called them, came in. He nodded to each and asked for James Whiteley. When James indicated that he was James, he announced, "I have a telegram from Scotland for you, that was received a few days ago, but because of the storm, we weren't able to deliver."

Immediately James took a look at the telegram and read it aloud,

'A Mr. & Mrs. Bartlett will be coming the first week in March to collect the Taylor children. The doctor indicated that they would be well enough to travel at that time.'

"Meg is going to be devastated," said Louise, adding, "but she did expect something like this,"

"I will go over and tell her before we leave," answered James motioning to Louise to follow him. Together, they exited the house waving goodbye to Liz and Bill. Louise had been smiling and looking better but now she was wearing a frown. James noted that and looked askance.

"Meg knows and is okay with that, but March is a very unpredictable time of year to be travelling in this part of the country?"

"To be sure, but let's just leave it for now and see what transpires, shall we?"

Christmas

As Christmas approached, Louise began to feel anxious. The weather had not been very stable and she felt strongly that she was going to be housebound over the season. She hated to admit it, but she was not feeling herself at all. At one time she thought she should mention this to James, however, he was so enthusiastic about the pageant that she didn't.

James had called for the neighbors to pitch in and make this pageant the best ever. They were so excited about it. All except Louise, she just couldn't get the least bit excited, although she never let on. Two weeks before Christmas, Louise got quite sick and James began to worry about her. He watched the weather constantly, hoping that it would hold or at least be calm. He vowed that he should take Louise into town, just to be sure and broached that to her. She was adamant that she should be with him over Christmas at least and wouldn't even talk about it.

The next day they had a caller. He wanted to talk to James ignoring Louise. She was not enthused with this man. He called himself a minister and introduced himself as Rev. Plitt. James welcomed him and asked Louise to make some tea for them, although they had just finished breakfast.

Where did he come from at this time of the morning, Louise wondered? Not only that, why did he come here and what does he want with James. She was not impressed with him at all and felt suspicious, but decided to keep quiet. She made tea and added some biscuits and jam, but refused to sit at the table with them when James requested it. He looked askance at her, but let it go.

They briefly discussed the new church or rather school and the reverend wanted to know if they were planning on hiring a minister. James very carefully explained that the government would be involved in the building of a school addition that could be used as a church on Sunday, in the beginning. It would depend on the head of the church, when or if a church was actually built here in the country or even in Lashburn. They discussed several things, weather was not one of them and neither was the country. It was a strange discussion and James started to feel negatively about this man. He refused to extend an invitation to stay for dinner and actually made an excuse for himself and Louise, saying they were invited to the neighbors for a luncheon. After he left, James bowed and begged forgiveness for telling a lie. Normally, James would talk until he found out more about the person, but in this case, he felt the same as Louise and could not get rid of that feeling.

Louise came over to him, and actually hugged him saying, "I don't know what it was about that man, but he was not a minister, of that I am sure. We need to watch him in any case. Perhaps we should go to the neighbors, for that very reason. I do have an unhealthy feeling,"

"Very well, we will do just that. I will get the team ready. The weather is not too bad, so travelling should be okay. Make sure you dress warm, my love," he answered.

They were ready in less than an hour and made off for the nearest neighbors. When they drove into the yard they found the visitor had already made himself known to them as well and was just leaving. It would be interesting to know what they thought of him.

They were always welcomed at the Bannister's. It was a such a happy home. The children were adorable and pulled at Louise' heart strings. She smiled as she spoke to each one.

When James joined her inside, they both asked about the visitor. It was Mrs. Bannister that spoke up, "I have never known such a rude man. He literally ignored me while he questioned my husband about different things."

"What did he ask about?" asked James directing the question to Bob Bannister.

"He was asking about the new church, and if we had a minister?"

"I told him, it was only in the idea stage, and that nothing had been determined to date. He needed to talk to you. But of course, he had already been to see you. We don't know too much about him, do we?" Bob asked.

"No we don't, and Louise feels very suspicious, and as a matter of fact, so am I." added James.

"Strange that someone would be coming around at this time of year and in this weather," said Mrs. Bannister.

"True, what was he really after?" answered James.

"We will ask in town. Perhaps they will have heard something. We will go to town tomorrow, as long as the weather holds and see what we can find out," reiterated James firmly.

"Good, then that's that and we will have tea. I put the kettle on when I saw you pull in. We are glad to see you both," clamored Mrs. Bannister.

When Louise and James got ready to leave, Mrs. Bannister, handed Louise a loaf of bread, one, with fruit and spices in it. It smelled heavenly and Louise accepted the gift with gratitude.

On the way home, James was in a solitary mood. Louise thought that perhaps he was mulling over our visitor. When he spoke, it was with that he had in mind, "Let's go to town tomorrow. I would like to talk to Liz and Bill and Meg and get their input on this stranger. Perhaps his real name, would help."

"I agree, and I would like to go to town myself. It will be a nice break," and with that she settled down in the sleigh and nodded off until she was awakened by James talking to the horses as they neared the farm.

The next day dawned sunny and clear, no sign of snow or wind. A good day to go to town thought Louise as she prepared the porridge for breakfast. She was thinking of what she needed to buy for sewing and thread and some material to work with. She was tired of tatting and had made enough lace for several outfits. As she made the tea, she absent-mindedly forgot to put the tea in the pot, so when she poured the tea it was only boiled water.

"Oh, dear, I've been dreaming again, sorry," she quickly said as she made to correct the mistake. James merely looked at her and smiled.

"It will do you good to go into town, me thinks," he said continuing to smile.

Within the hour, all was ready, dishes were washed and put away. Some coal was added to the stove wood, to keep it going until they came home. She added a scarf to her coat and mittens, which she had also made. She held up a pair for James, as he drew up to the door and called to her.

The drive into town was pleasant. They rode in silence most of the way. When they got to Liz', he dropped Louise off and continued to the barns to take care of the horses.

"Oh, I am so glad to see you," called Liz.

"I am glad to get out and about. It is pleasant outside and the drive was great, but I am ready for a cup of tea," she answered.

"Good, we can talk over the latest happenings,"

"What has happened?" asked Louise.

"Wait until James comes and I will tell you both,"

Louise couldn't wait for James, and said so.

"Oh well, a man came in looking for James. He didn't give me his name or why he was here, but Bill was watching him and declared that he had seen him before. He thought about it and finally remembered that a man had been looking for a job a while back and at that time, when they asked where he lived, he ignored the question. They watched him and he went toward the native grounds. Bill wasn't really sure but believed he had been living with the natives. Bill didn't trust him and told me to watch out and not to rent a room to him. He didn't ask for one and disappeared soon after having some tea and biscuits without paying. We told the Mounties about him. He may be harmless but you never know.

"He was at our place, asking about the church we are going to build, and did we have a minister?"

"He doesn't appear to be a minister, in my eyes," said Liz.

At that moment James came in the door and noting the looks on the two women, knew something was up. He greeted Liz and asked for Bill.

"He is out getting some firewood,"

"I could've helped him," replied James

"Oh, he's got help. The children were so excited to go on the sleigh with him, they came in early all dressed up for the cold. We just love those little guys,"

"Good, the fresh air will do them good,"

"Oh, Meg had been going the extra mile to make sure they are healthy and doing such a good job,"

"Tell him about the man, you mentioned, Liz?"

Liz repeated what she told Louise earlier. James merely sat there thinking. He looked at Louise and smiled. "Bill had good instincts and I would say he is probably right. We will just have to make it known to the neighbors, to keep an eye open and watch out for him. Reporting it is a good thing Liz, I thank you,"

"Louise if you want to go to the General Store, you can. I will wait for you here,"

"Right, I will be back as soon as I can."

Louise took off in a hurry. She was on a mission. Now was her opportunity to order what she needed for Christmas presents. There wasn't much time left so she wanted it soon. While she was standing there ordering, she felt faint and clutched at the counter for support. The Manager noting this, ran to her side and helped her to a seat. He noted she was sweating, and pale. He called to a young helper to go to Liz's and get James, something was not right with Louise who was trying to sit up but her body wasn't cooperating.

James rushed in, along with Liz and Bill.

"Louise are you alright?" James asked. She just nodded and nearly fell off her chair in a faint.

"When does the doctor come next?" he asked Liz.

"He should be coming the beginning of next week. James, I would like to keep her at my place until then," she looked worried and James noted that.

"Oh, I think that would be the thing to do," he answered. "I truly believe she needs some good rest. You know her, she is busy doing ten things at once. I have never known anyone like her," James added and knelt down beside Louise.

"My, darling, I want you to stay with Liz, until the doctor comes next week. It is important that you take it easy. I will go home now and come back tomorrow. I must take care of the horses but I will pray that you will be okay."

Louise just nodded and smiled. She just wanted to lay down. Liz took charge and asked Bill to help get Louise to her place and bed. Louise only nodded to James, blowing him a kiss, then closing her eyes.

Liz and Bill got Louise settled in bed, with a promise to check on her later. It wasn't long, when Liz checked, she found Louise fast asleep.

"I am worried about her, she looks played out," remarked Liz.

"I noticed that too, but I don't think James would let her overdo it,"

"I believe she is worrying about this baby, because of what happened to Meg. All we can do is reinforce the fact that all is well,"

"I am glad she was here when that happened. James wouldn't know what to do and would worry," added Bill.

"You go on to bed, I still have some things to do in the kitchen, and I will check on her later, and maybe during the night,"

"Okay, I am tired, but I can do some checking in the night, to relieve you."

"It's all right. It will be on my mind anyway. Sleep will avoid me, I am afraid."

"Yes, my dear, I figured that," and with that he toddled off to bed. It had been a tough evening.

Liz puttered in the kitchen for the next hour or so, and then decided to check on Louise.

"My goodness, you are awake." she said as she peeked in the door.

"Yes, but could I get up and have a cup of tea. I feel like I haven't eaten today?'

"It is possible; you did not eat when you came in. What did you have for breakfast?"

"A cup of tea, I didn't feel like eating. Funny, I normally am always hungry,"

"Well, I will get you tea and something to eat, and we will sit and chat,"

"Good," Louise stated as she proceeded to get up, but sat right back down in a hurry. She looked confused.

"I seem to be light headed," she said shakily.

"You just stay right there, I will bring it to you, my dear," stated Liz.

Liz went to the kitchen, but frowned at what just happened. I'm going to send for Dr. Taylor. With her mind made up she proceeded to make a biscuit with jam and tea, adding some cookies as well. When she entered the bedroom, Louise was fast asleep. Alarmed, Liz nudged her and spoke softly,

"Here is your tea, now can you sit up?"

Louise opened her eyes and spotted the cups, sitting up saying,

"Did I doze off again?" Liz just nodded set a pillow behind Louise and sat down beside her. She had made herself a cup of tea as well. They sat comfortably for a few moments, savoring the tea. Louise sighed, saying, " I know I have been worrying about getting caught in a snow storm and confined to the farm. James would be frantic, I know. And I have been moody and listless. I need to ask Dr. Taylor about it."

"I am sending for the doctor, in the morning, by the way, and I agree," added Liz.

"Thank you, you are a true friend," as she yawned and motioned that she wanted to lie down again.

"Go back to sleep, Louise. I will check on you later, but I will not disturb you until morning, Goodnight, my dear. You are also a true friend and I thank you," Liz replied as she hugged Louise and covered her up. Liz felt tears, so she quickly turned out the light and left with the tray.

Louise slept through the night, but awoke with a start early in the morning disoriented. She couldn't make out where she was, "Oh, dear, what is the matter with me," she murmured.

Liz heard her talking and quickly got up and ran to her bedroom.

"Louise, you are at my place, don't you remember?"

"Oh, yes, it's coming back. I was dreaming that I was back home in my bedroom, and I couldn't quite figure why my bed was so big. You see I only had a single bed back home, in a rather small bedroom. My mother had made lovely curtains and a bed quilt for me. I do miss my family!" she said shedding a tear.

Liz felt so sorry for her, " Come you need a cup of tea to wake you up. Remember you are carrying your own family?"

"Thanks, yes and I am really happy, just worried about it,"

"The doctor will be here soon and that will settle your mind, or it should,"

"Yes, it will. I feel sorry to put James through all of this," she said and sighed.

"Come now, he understands and is very concerned about you,"

"I know, and I love him dearly," and with that statement, she put on a robe that Liz loaned her and slowly walked out into the dining area and the morning sunshine.

"Oh, how lovely!" Louise stated and sat down at a table by a window, so she could look outside.

When James came in the next day, Louise decided she would wait for the doctor and if all is well go home with him and made no bones about it. James agreed to leave her there for a few days until that happened. He had planned a meeting of the neighbors to talk about the Christmas pageant but he did not say anything to Louise, otherwise he knew she would not stay in town at all.

Two days later, Dr. Taylor came in and when he saw Meg's face, he knew something was bothering her.

"Okay, what is it?" he asked as he entered the door.

"Louise is at Liz's and she wants to see you. I don't think she has been feeling that well and collapsed at the General Store three days ago. I am concerned that she is worried because of my little episode," she said all in one breath.

"Relax, I will go over there and take a look at her. She is a healthy young woman," he answered.

"Great, let me know, will you? Before I go crazy. I can't keep focused on the children today," she said as she sighed.

"Don't worry."

Dr. Taylor picked up his bag and headed over to Liz's, without waiting for his regular cup of tea. When he arrived, Liz was openly relieved.

"I will talk to Louise in the bedroom," he announced after greeting Liz.

"Louise, tell me what has been happening to you?"

An hour later, he came out of the bedroom and declared his patient was as fit as anyone he knew, but she must take it easy. She tells me she is going back to the farm as soon as possible. A little hypertension I suspect as a result of witnessing Meg's crisis, is her only problem. Everything else is normal. At that Liz gave a huge sigh of relief.

"Please, tell Meg, I know she is worried."

"I will, and how about you. How are you feeling?" the doctor asked.

"Oh me? Why I am just fine, thank you, and now relieved," she answered.

"Then I will be going, and I will be here until tomorrow. Meg will put me up for the night, so I can see a couple more patients before I return. Meg will send word to me if anything else develops with Louise."

After she saw the doctor, Louise was ready and waiting for James adamant about going home after all she was only in the first stages of her term.

"I guess I just worry too much!" she said.

Chapter Eleven

The Pageant

After weeks of practicing, they were all ready for Christmas and looking forward to the pageant. Christmas eve the children and adults gathered at the neighbors, who had a good sized barn that had been cleaned and benches and a stage added. Louise and James had been there all day, making sure all was ready. Being busy was helping Louise.

The children were also there practicing their lines between giggles watching the donkey, a goat and a lamb brought in for the stage setting. The lamb fell asleep on the stage and the donkey and goat, chewed away contentedly beside the stage.

People arrived bringing goodies for lunch. It was going to be quite an evening. Louise was happy just being there watching the activities trying hard to ignore the barn odors.

James, started the event, at precisely seven o'clock, greeting everyone and asking them to sit down and enjoy, saying, "We will begin by singing, 'Oh, Come All Ye Faithful, and then the children will recite the story."

They began and without missing a word told the story as it was in the Bible, often looking at the animals, who were oblivious to the attention they were receiving. A huge applause came at the end, after which James asked them to stand and sing a couple more carols. Everyone joined in singing loudly as well as Louise who was wishing she had a piano at this time but never the less enjoyed it.

They ended the evening giving out candy, apples and an orange each to the youngsters and the smell of coffee permeated the barn. Louise had not smelled that since the wagon train and it made her smile at the thought. James caught her smiling and looked askance, but she just nodded and smiled, with that 'I will tell you later' look.

The evening was a success. Not only that, Ian and Mary had been able to join the children and were the centre of attention afterwards. They were so happy. Meg and John, thanked Louise and James profusely." Ian and Mary will remember this as long as they live, even though they will be thousands of miles away, I know," Meg said with emphasis.

"I also thank you. What Meg said is so true. It is also a great tribute to the Church," John said.

"Amen," chorused Louise and James. Those who were standing nearby, heard what was said and they too, joined in.

The evening ended with a grand luncheon and soon everyone was bundling up their children and heading for home. Outside the men, were getting the horses and sleighs ready. James, of course, had the bells on his team and you could hear them for miles as they made their way home. Louise was feeling much better.

"James, that was just wonderful," she said with so much love in her eyes.

"Thank you, my love. I am happy we could do this for the people. It is such a hard life out here. They deserve this, and so do we," he said happily, as the horses trotted and the bells rang out.

"God Bless everyone," he added noting that Louise was nodding off. Suddenly she asked, "How did John and Meg get there?"

James let out a laugh, "John brought them out for Christmas. The house is almost finished, but he wanted them to have Christmas at the farm and planned it. The children were thrilled. This will be their last Christmas here in Canada, perhaps forever, who knows?"

"They will be back, because there is so much love there," she answered sleepily.

Christmas

Christmas Day came and went very quietly in the Whiteley household. Louise of course, prepared a lovely dinner and they both exchanged gifts. James however, explained that he had one extra gift but it was too big to bring out to the farm. However, he promised Louise that it would be waiting at Liz's, the next time they went to town. Louise could not imagine what it was and begged James to tell her, but he would not and told her to be patient.

The weather turned cold Christmas Day and remained that way for up to two months. James and Louise managed to stay healthy the whole time but always wished for a break. John and Meg had moved back to town on Christmas Day. The house was just a little too cold for them they said, but the children had loved every minute of it.

When the weather did break, James decided to ready the team and told Louise to dress warmly for the ride into town. He realized the isolation was hard on Louise and felt she needed a break.

She did as she was told, without question, this time. In her heart, she knew that it was the fact that she did not have people to look after or any projects she could do at the time. Daylight hours were short and she needed supplies. James wanted her to stay with Liz for a while. She would worry about him, he knew. He had spent a winter here before she arrived, so he understood the deepening silence out in the country, the long evenings and especially the cold. It was important to keep the fires going. Louise was adamant that she would only stay for a couple of weeks for a break. She needed to visit with the women and get more supplies and that's what she did. That's why she was in town when in the middle of March, a south wind blew and warmed the earth. Little rivulets formed everywhere. Though it was slushy, everyone was out and about. Louise was afraid of slipping and falling. She did not want anything to happen to this child. James joined her at Liz's. He was glad she had been in town at least for a little while.

As they were settling down for supper, a Mountie came in apologizing for the interruption. Liz was quick to question him and set another plate on the table. He thanked her and faced James, introducing himself as Sgt. Williams, saying grimly, "I have a telegram from Scotland, and it sounds like the couple is on their way to pick up the children."

Meg and the children had joined them for a meal and hearing the telegram she immediately got up from the table, saying, "I don't feel like eating," and left. The children were bewildered.

"This is not a good time for them to be coming, is it?" James queried.

"Right, I don't think they understand this country at all," the Mountie said.

"Meg has been preparing the children for this day, but still gets upset," James uttered.

"John as well, he will be devastated. He has been working so hard on the farm, just so the children can have a home in the country," Liz acknowledged.

"Well, we will pray that it all turns out alright. Louise has her own problem now but she will be good for Meg. Together, John and Meg will adjust and adapt," added James. He was thinking of his own child and how he would feel in this situation. It will be God's will, he thought to himself still thinking how thankful Louise was okay.

"We will be ready for them, and hope for the best," answered Liz.

The days flew by as the warming wind reduced the snow banks and showed bits of black earth visible. Of course, they also knew spring storms could sometimes be devastating. The people were accustomed to this and took great joy in days that were warm.

It was on one of these warm, slushy days that the couple from Scotland arrived, somewhat dismayed. They made a great clamor when they walked into Liz's café/inn, demanding assistance. They realized only after a few moments that it was not the thing to do when Liz approached them with fire in her eyes.

"If you think that you can come in here and expect to be treated like royalty, forget it. I am the proprietor and you will calm down and sit down. I will make you some tea and then we will talk," she spoke with emphasis. They could see that she was not happy at all. Both were dishevelled but dressed far too opulent. His eyes, which were dark above a nose that was almost buried in a bushy red beard, showed weariness and the woman also appeared tired but competent. Her greying hair was pulled back severely in a bun above a thin face.

"I am so sorry, we didn't mean to ....," she stopped when she saw a Mountie come in and nod to Liz than continued, "We have come a very long way, and have endured so much. No one told us about the weather in this country or that it was so big or that we had to come so far out of the big city," she said, slowly. Whereas Liz, suddenly realizing how tired they were relented saying,

"Come sit down and I will get you a bite to eat, if you wish. I can also put you up. You can have the downstairs bedroom. It was just vacated and has been cleaned,"

"Thank you, the lady finally spoke quietly introducing herself and her husband as the Cameron's," her dark eyes looking very weary.

"We are here to take the children back to Scotland," Mr. Cameron added

"I know, but you are going to have to learn somewhat about them first," said Liz.

The Mountie spoke up then, thanking Liz and adding, "I am Cpl. Harrison, here for that purpose, to make sure those children are treated properly. We will not release them otherwise and that is our law! I also would advise you to not go around demanding anything. The people here have come from your country and others and will definitely take it as an insult and that will not bode well,"

The couple both bowed their heads as Mr. Cameron said, " We weren't prepared for any of this. I am so sorry!" he said, gesturing with his hands.

They appeared to be really hungry, and gladly helped themselves to scones and tea, requesting another cup. They retired after thanking Liz. She quietly informed them about breakfast adding then we will talk. The Mountie indicated to them that he would be there for a few days.

"They don't have proper hats or boots? I will find some for them and see if they will use them? That's a very expensive fur coat Mrs. Cameron is wearing? It should be warm enough but the shoes?" Liz spoke to the Mountie.

He nodded to Liz and then asked for a room for the next two nights after saying he would be back later. He had some other things to do. He didn't say what it was, which made Liz wonder what was going on. She usually was on top of it all. She would have to keep her ears open and eyes keen.

When Bill came through the door, with a 'what's going on' expression, she quickly filled him in.

" I think it might be a good idea to ride out and tell James and John. I don't know about you, but they look pretty posh to me. I think they should be taken out to the farm to see just where those children were raised and what it is truly like. Get rid of that high strung idea, that they are going to rush right back with those children in tow," said Liz.

"You're a might stirred up, young lady, better calm down," Bill could always talk her down.

"Will you be able to ride out in the morning?" she asked.

"After I talk to the Mountie, yes." he said.

"What is he after?" Liz questioned, noting something in Bill's voice, that bothered her.

"I am not quite sure, he was questioning the General Store Manager and some of the people walking around, including me, just general questions," he replied.

"We will probably know tomorrow. He is a very nice chap."

Bill nodded towards the bedroom. " I am tired, love, could we call it a day?"

"Yup, I just have a couple of things to do and I will be right behind you."

Morning dawned bright, highlighting the water dripping off the eaves. No one had moved and Liz, as usual was busy preparing the breakfast menu. She hummed as she worked and

Bill smiled as he finished dressing and joined her. She was such an uplifting person, but mind you, she also had some fire in her. He loved her so much and proceeded to let her know that. As they were hugging, the Mountie appeared, freshly shaved and smiling calling a cheery, "Good Morning,"

"And a Good morning to you too," answered Bill and Liz together.

"It is a beautiful sunny morning, and please sit, I will get your breakfast, "said Liz with a sheepish grin. *Caught, she thought, but I don't care. That man is precious.*

It wasn't two minutes until a grumpy voice called out, "Is breakfast ready? I didn't sleep too well. What in the blazes was that howling?"

"That's our local woodsmen singing," replied Bill. The Mountie just lowered his head, and looked away and burst out laughing. "They are coyotes, and will howl some nights, but we are all used to it. Sorry that they had to do it last night, but some people say it's a change in the weather," described the Cpl.

"Oh, it is an eerie sound, and my wife couldn't settle, worrying about it. She will be here after fussing with her hair," Mr. Cameron stated.

"No problem, sit thee down," said Liz. She could just smack Bill for his explanation of the coyotes, but it was funny and she had to smile to herself. Mr. Cameron obviously didn't think it so.

"I have had my breakfast, so I am off to see James," Bill spoke specifically to the Mountie.

"If you wait a bit, I will join you. I would like to talk to both James and John and take note where they live,"

"Okay," replied Bill.

"Could we go along too?" Mr. Cameron asked.

"I don't think you are up to horseback riding?" Bill mentioned.

"Oh, but that's where you are wrong, we both ride,"

"Right then, I will see about getting two horses for you, and Liz has found some boots and jackets for you both to wear. This is not country for fur coats and fancy hats. The natives might think you were animals and use their bow and arrow."

Mr. Cameron looked quite chagrinned. He motioned to his wife when she entered the room, all dressed up in a long dress and small fancy hat. Liz just lifted her eyebrows and asked her to sit down and have some breakfast.

"I don't really eat breakfast, just some tea," she said quietly.

"My lady, in this country, you better learn to eat while you can because it will be awhile before you get another chance," emphasized Liz. That's when Mr. Cameron told his wife they would be riding out into the country. Liz has brought us jackets and boots to wear. This is wild country, I understand and we might encounter Indians.

"Oh, no, is that what I heard last night?" his wife looked at him wide-eyed.

"No, but I will explain to you, later. Right now do eat something, and then change for goodness sake. The Mountie has gone to get two horses for us. He will be riding out with us and the other gentleman, I didn't get his name," he said looking at Liz.

"That's my husband, Bill, and yes he will be riding out with you. I don't think any of you would find it on your own. The roads are mere rutted trails," she explained.

At that point, Mrs. Cameron did sit down and readily drank a cup of tea, but failed to eat anything else.

The two of them changed, but Mrs. Cameron, still wore a long dress. Well thought Liz, she will have to ride side-saddle, probably trained that way, as she wandered back to the kitchen after giving them the clothes. The look on their faces when she gave them the clothes was hilarious. She would have to tell Bill about it later. She also wished that she could warn Louise and James.

When the men rode up to the door, they were waiting. Mr. Cameron was not as patient as his wife. He was pacing back and for in front of the hotel(house), or rundown shack as he called it when no one could hear.

"What kind of a horse is this?" he asked when they stopped.

"Just get on the horse, and quite complaining. People here will think you're some kind of royalty," Bill said.

They both got on the horses. Mrs. Cameron, did indeed ride side saddle. Her dress would not allow anything else, however she said nothing, just nodding and giving her husband a look of disgust.

The four of them started out slowly and then picked up speed, as the horses picked their way along the trail. There were still some drifts in the shaded areas. The sun was bright with no wind, so it really was a glorious day to be travelling. The Cpl. and Bill were chatting, while Mr. Cameron simply grunted once in a while. Finally, he asked how far it was going to be.

"We should be there in about 20 minutes," the Mountie told them.

"That long? My wife is getting tired."

"Relax and enjoy the countryside," said Bill, trying desperately to ease the situation. Mr. Cameron asked again about the children living all this time in this forlorn place.

"Oh, no, they were living in town, but Meg and John decided that they should see their old home before they leave because that is where their parents are buried," answered Bill.

"Is Meg the one that has been looking after them?" the lady asked, coming alert suddenly.

"Meg, and what a job, she has done. The children love her," replied Bill.

"Well, she will be relieved of her duty soon," Mrs. Cameron responded.

"Yes, but to her it was not a duty. The children needed someone to love them and care for them or they too would have succumbed to the disease." Bill was getting tired of their inference.

"We are coming into the yard of their home. This is where they lived,"

"Oh God forbid, that is nothing but a shack. Who could ever live there?"

"It is looking a little dilapidated right now, but it was their home,"

"You can just make out the crosses on their graves at the back of the house."

Mrs. Cameron looked stunned and bowed her head when she saw the partly visible crosses in the snow.

"John and Meg and the children recently moved to the farm, just a little farther on the other side of the road. James lives a half mile to the north of John. We will be there shortly," Bill nodded to the Mountie.

They turned the horses and proceeded to John's place, where smoke was billowing out of the chimney. When they rode up to the door, Meg came out smiling a greeting, "Hello, and welcome to our home," she said.

"These are Mr. & Mrs. Cameron, the people who are taking the children back to Scotland, "Come in, we have been expecting you and the children are excited,"

Bill was apprehensive and looked it, but when John came out, he relaxed when he saw two eager little faces, standing behind him. The Cpl. smiled at them. What a sight they were, so happy and full of life.

"It is a shame that they have to be uprooted. They have been through a lot and Meg and John have given them so much," Bill said.

Mr. Cameron spoke hastily as he entered the house again telling him that it was their duty.

The house was warm and cozy. The kettle was whistling on the stove. Everything was spotless and tidy, even though all the furniture was hand hewn. Meg was to be admired for what she had done with the Soddy.

Bill and the Mountie were watching Mrs. Cameron, she seemed to be a little in shock. She kept looking around and when asked to sit, dusted the chair off before sitting down. Meg served tea and scones with jam and cream. It smelled heavenly, but there was no acknowledgement from the Cameron's. Mr. Cameron ate, but his wife merely sipped at her tea.

Suddenly Cpl. Harrison, asked where the children had gone to? We saw them when we came in."

"Oh, they are here, but noticed the strangers and well, they are afraid of leaving," answered Meg.

"I can understand that, but I would like to talk to them."

"Come out, children. You aren't going anywhere," called Meg.

The two of them came out from behind a curtain, wide eyed and quiet.

"Come and meet Mr. & Mrs. Cameron from Scotland. I want you to get to know them."

Both replied, "It's nice to meetcha," and ran back behind the curtain.

"Why are they so shy?" asked Mrs. Cameron.

"Are you not used to children?" asked John, now becoming alarmed.

"I suggest we go have a talk with James. He was the last person, Ian talked to,"

Cpl. Harrison interjected.

"Good idea," said John, adding, "and I'll come with you. I need to see James as well."

They quickly finished their tea and donned their coats. Mrs. Cameron still had hers on and was the first one out the house, muttering to herself. John, who was closest to her, heard and looked askance. When she realized he had heard her, she quickly turned and mounted her horse without any assistance. He noted that and nodded to Bill, who had been watching every move.

It only took fifteen minutes to ride over to James. He was at the door to welcome them, when they arrived. Louise stood behind him with a somewhat lesser welcome. They were invited in, where Louise had already laid out a table with pastries and tea. Mrs. Cameron looked amazed when she entered and smiled. The place was quite fascinating, but so small. When Louise realized what she thought, she spoke up saying, "All homes in the country are small. We don't have the comforts that you have been used to. However, there is not a home in this area that doesn't have a lot of love. We deal with the wildness, the inconveniences and work hard and God is with us all the way. The children have been witness to this, but have progressed and become so endearing to us all. We hate to see them go,"

"I did not know, this country even existed until ten days ago, and I can perhaps understand somewhat how difficult it has been for people,"

Louise felt that she was warming up a little. However, she never mentioned the children and she knew she met them. Curious. She caught James's eye then, but remained quiet only asking them to sit down and have tea with them.

"Try some scones," said Bill as he reached for one himself, "Louise is one of the best bakers in this country and the best seamstress.'

That raised the Cameron's eyes. "Seamstress, you say?" questioned Mr. Cameron.

James spoke up then, ignoring his question asking both for some identification as to who they were and the letter that was supposed to identify them. Both understood.

"Oh, the letter, is back at that place where we stayed. We can get it to you," he added, looking at Cpl. Harrison for direction who asked, "Can you come to town tomorrow, James? Perhaps we can settle that then."

"Yes, I can do that. I will also ask Meg to bring the children along with their baggage. She has been preparing them for this day,"

"Good, I would like to look over the information as well," the Mountie spoke also suggesting, "Mrs. Cameron, please get acquainted with the children. If they are going to be in your care, I need to know they are safe,"

"I will and we should be leaving soon. They are expecting us back home," she said with much ado.

"You need to think more about the children than what they want back home," replied Louise, getting quite disturbed at what she was hearing. She paced back and forth, while she listened.

Then James spoke up saying, "If the children are not comfortable travelling with you, we will take action to keep them here,"

Both Cameron's seemed a little subdued over that last statement. Mr. Cameron vowed to carry out orders from Scotland and Mrs. Cameron was to care for the children. As he spoke to the group, his eyes kept sweeping between James and the Mountie.

"We best be getting back," Bill, who had been very quiet, spoke up.

"Yes, they called in unison," starting to put their coats and hats on once more.

It was a quiet trip back to town, with Bill leading the way.

"I understand now, why you wanted us to come out here. It was to really get to know where the children lived and how," Mr. Cameron said. Mrs. Cameron, however, said nothing. She did not fit the child minder description that was first mentioned in the letter.

Back at the boarding house, all was quiet as they ate their supper. Everyone was perhaps trying to think of a way to keep the children, but knowing also that it was hopeless.

Bedtime couldn't come soon enough for the Cameron's; they were dog tired to say the least. Liz noted that Mrs. Cameron did not seem too happy and she only picked at her supper. She got a feeling that something did not seem right and wondered what Louise thought of Mrs. Cameron. It wasn't long before everyone was in their room and all was quiet. Liz and Bill sat for a time, going over the day's events.

"I hope Louise and James come in tomorrow along with Meg and John and the children," said Liz with that hopeful look on her face.

"I have a feeling that they will, if only for Meg and John's sake," answered Bill.

"I believe that Mountie is watching closely," added Liz.

"I have a strange feeling that he has suspicions, but isn't saying anything. He may have been in touch with Scotland,"

"Bedtime, my love, it's been a long day,"

"Right, I'll be right in," replied Liz, walking back to the kitchen to blow out the lamp.

Meanwhile back at the Whiteley's, Louise was wondering what to do, while she got breakfast ready. She wanted to go along with James to say goodbye to the children, although she was not feeling that great. James would go along with that she was sure. He was always busy outside doing his chores. He seemed to like working with horses, she mused.

He came in shortly taking off his boots and coat and clapping his hands to warm them up. Louise wrinkled her nose at him saying, "You smell like horses," and laughed when she finished.

"I like working with horses, they listen, but don't answer, "he said.

"Your breakfast is ready. I want to go with you to town. I believe Meg, John and the children are going in this morning."

"Of course, dress warm. I'll get the sleigh ready right after we eat."

"Good I'll be ready," Louise said.

The sleigh ride into town was joyful. Both were contented listening to the bells as the horses trotted along. Liz was at the door waiting to welcome them saying," Meg, John and the children are on their way."

"The Cameron's are still in their room and the Mountie has been out and about all morning," replied Bill.

As he was speaking a great hustle and bustle was heard at the door and in came James, Meg, John and two boisterous children who quickly ran to Louise with hugs.

"Slow down you two, remember why we are here," called Meg.

The Cameron's entered the dining room then and expressed their good mornings. Mrs. Cameron asked Louise quietly if she could talk to her and Meg privately.

"Of course, we will go into the bedroom," answered Louise.

"First of all, please call me Margaret. I am Jack's wife, but I am not the child minder they were supposed to send for the children. I don't have children of my own, but I can assure you that I will do everything in my power to see that they arrive safely in Scotland. Their grandmother, can be domineering, but I do believe she has their welfare at heart. We will be able to explain where they were living and how distant it was and where their parents are buried. I do know that Ian had a disagreement with his mother before they left. I don't know what it was over, but I do know that his mother was very upset at the time. I hope all this makes sense to you both," she said lowering her head.

Meg spoke up while Louise nodded," We are both glad that you did speak up. Your husband can be kind of brash and we were worried about letting the children go, when you are stranger to them. Please get to know them. They are precious to John and we have worked so hard to help them heal from more than one aspect."

"Meg is right, I am also glad you spoke up, and it does make a difference to all of us and though we did not know the Taylor's very well, they were neighbors and in this country, neighbors are important," added Louise.

"Thank you both for being so kind and please I apologize for us," Mrs. Cameron uttered.

They joined the rest for tea and goodies. The men were enjoying a lively conversation. It was good to see Mr. Cameron warming up and joining in the light hearted talk and constantly including the children in the chatter. The children were also beginning to answer questions without fear.

"Our bags are all packed," said young Ian and Mary chimed in, "we are ready to take on the world," which made everyone laugh. It was a bitter-sweet goodbye. Louise noted that John and Meg sat in silence the whole time.

"I would like to offer a prayer before you go," said James and everyone bowed their heads and joined in on the Lord's prayer at the end.

"Thank you very much," echoed the Cameron's

The children suddenly were subdued realizing that this was goodbye. They started to cry but when they looked at Meg, quietened down and with their chins held high marched out with the Cameron's on the way to Scotland and goodness knows what.

Everyone was waving and calling, "We love you."

Meg and John remained in the house along with Liz and Bill standing in silence when James spoke up, "I pray that all will be well and that someday we will see them again." On the way home he said to Louise, "I have never seen such a change in attitude before, I will keep praying for those children."

The Baby

The weather warmed and the work on the farm continued. James with the help of Bill put the crop in and planned a small garden for Louise to hoe. The sewing never stopped either, as people learned of Louise genius with patterns. Although she was getting heavier every day, she managed to keep up with everyday chores. Meg came over often to keep her company and help out. They were becoming very close friends and made the trip into town to visit with Liz as often as possible. As the days went by Louise became edgy and James sensed the hot summer weather might be bothering her. He got excited when Louise announced that she felt the baby kick. He just kept smiling.

Louise knew that fall wasn't far away and she would have to have help. It would be hard with a baby to look after as well. In the meantime, Louise had prepared bottles of soup and canned meat. She decided there was no way the bread she made would keep so she asked Mrs. Bannister to help while she was away. It was also something she could do after the baby came.

When Louise finally gave in and went to Liz's she settled into a routine but kept working in the kitchen. Liz watched her and noticed that she was slowing down and would stop and rest often. August was approaching and James came in often to check on Louise. Before the end of the month, she went into labor and the doctor was called. Liz called Meg to come and help, because she was afraid the doctor would not get there in time and she was not a mid-wife. Meg wasn't either but was not afraid to assist the doctor when he needed help. The two women put her to bed and kept watch.

The labor lasted twenty-four hours and Louise groaned a little louder each time. The doctor arrived just as she let out a scream. He quickly washed and got to work with Meg assisting.

A little girl was born sometime later. Mother and baby were tucked into bed and both were asleep when James came bursting in. He was met with smiles and greetings on being a father. He rushed to the bedroom and stopped short at what he saw, a mother with a baby in her arms, resting quietly. He immediately dropped down beside the bed and prayed, tears spilling down his face. He turned to the others, saying, "I am so grateful that all is well,"

"You are the proud father of a healthy baby girl," the doctor said smiling.

A cheer went up in the kitchen where Liz was preparing some tea. She announced she was planning a special supper for all in celebration of the event. They were all excited.

The doctor asked Meg to go with him to the office to see his other patients, then he said he would come back and look in on Louise. She is exhausted but the baby needs nourishment he told them. Meg informed him that she looked in and the baby was already feeding.

"Then all is well," he answered.

Liz had given James a bed and soon all was quiet until Bill came bounding in, carrying water. He called asking what was going on?" only to be told by Liz to shush! "This has been one heck of a day, if you must know. Where have you been all this time?"

"We had trouble with the well. I am tired but I need a good hot cup of tea or soup or something."

"Coming right up, sit thee down,"

"You are a good woman," he said looking at her lovingly.

Liz could see Bill was beginning to close his eyes, and that to her was a sign that he was very tired. "Go to bed, my dear. I have some work to do in the kitchen and I want to look in on Louise. I will be up later,"

After tea next day, all went their separate ways. James sat with Louise and the baby for a time and then decided he had better go home while it was still day light. Before he left however, he asked Louise about a name. She had been thinking about it too.

"I would like to name her Elizabeth," she said.

"Good, then that is what it shall be. My little girl, Betty or Beth, whatever. Oh, I almost forgot, there is a present for you in the front room," he said nodding.

"What in the world is it?" she asked.

Liz shouted just then, "It is the most wonderful thing I have ever heard," fingering the keys.

"Oh, James, a piano?" She could not believe it but was thrilled and couldn't wait to play it.

"It has taken a while to get here and I wanted to surprise you," he said smiling broadly.

As the days flew by, and Louise gained her strength back, she was determined to return to their home on the farm. James was only too glad to accommodate. The trip home was wonderful for Louise. She always loved the fall and the changes in vegetation and most of all the fresh air and baby Elizabeth slept the whole time. The only disappointment was they had to leave the piano behind.

James was only to happy to them back to the farm. He was so proud of his daughter; and couldn't help smiling. He told everyone he saw that he was a proud father of a beautiful baby girl. Louise was excited to return home and get back to work. She knew that the fall work was just beginning and would be busy.

At home James asked Louise to sit after she put the baby to bed. "I was at the stable today and they are looking for someone to take over the management of it. Seems there are a lot more people arriving in the spring and the present manager is planning on leaving at that time. If you don't mind I would like that job, I am not a farmer and I know that the house where Meg lived is now vacant. What do you think of us moving there?"

"James, I will go wherever you go, you know that. Yes, I would love to be in town. There I can sew to my heart's content. It will be easier on us.

"When you mentioned Meg, I wonder how they are making out? They will miss those children I am sure, "cried Louise.

"Yes, we can pray for them, time will heal but memories will last forever,"

"God Bless them for all that they have done for those children. I believe they will never forget them."

To which Louise nodded in agreement and closed her eyes in prayer.

Chapter Twelve

Moving To Lashburn

There was more planning to do now that we too will be moving though it was not that far away. Louise couldn't agree more on the fact that James was not a farmer. He tried so hard, but his heart was not in it. She could feel the frustration when he tried to mend some of the harness and some of the machinery, even though he did not complain. Bill probably felt the same way. John seems to be the true farmer. He could fix almost anything and seemed to understand the land better than all of them. It will be so much easier for us, too, she thought and started exploring ideas in her mind.

"Betty or Elizabeth, you are going to grow up in Lashburn, Saskatchewan. It will be a mouthful for you to learn. I can teach you to play the piano too. What do you think of that?" she said as she held the baby close to her heart and sang quietly, lulling her to sleep yet again.

"Must be the fresh air, my little one," she crooned.

She was not paying any attention to James, who was sitting so quiet watching the pair, grinning to himself. He too was thinking about the move and what a relief it would be for him. He was tired and worried about the winter out on the prairie. It was so lonely and desolate. The only comfort, were the neighbors who came around frequently. Of course, Lashburn is not very far away, so visiting would continue, he was sure. Louise thrived on visiting and learning new ideas and it never ceased to amaze him.

And so another chapter in their lives would soon start and both of them looked forward, to new experiences so very different and far away from their childhood homes.

It would take the rest of the year to do the harvesting and sell the farm and make the move into town. Of course, James got the job and they were both ecstatic about it.

There was so much to do first Louise knew. She would have to think about what she really wanted to move. They would need the beds, her dresser and of course the large stove that James had purchased but they could leave the small one that was there in the first place and oh, yes, the crib. Betty would use it for a time yet, however she wanted another child and soon. She believed children should not grow up alone, as she had gaining a little brother when she was so much older.

Her piano had recently been moved to the school house. Liz needed the room at the inn. Louise was fine with that but hoped that eventually she could have it at home. She liked playing and wanted to teach Betty.

"I know that you have applied for a minister full time, but what about a church. We have not heard from Rev. Lloyd about it and he did promise. Perhaps, you need to write a letter telling him about all the people that are coming to this area daily," Louise asked James.

"You are right, my love. I will tell you what to write, if you will do that for me?"

They had also been discussing what they needed to do at the house, before moving in and what they needed to take. Later that night, after the baby was fed and bathed and put to bed, she wrote the letter for James to sign and mail.

"I have packed up all my preserves and clothes that I don't need at the moment,"

"Good, but first I have to do some work or rather John and Bill will do some work on the house. It needs some extra sawdust in the walls and Meg said it needed some upgrading. Let me check it out and I will give you a time. I would like to take the crop off and sell the grain. It will give us a start in town. The horses, I will keep at the stable for my own use," and with that he got ready for bed.

Louise realized suddenly that she was bombarding him with questions, when he was still working hard on the farm. She must be patient. Summer was filled with preserving, forever watching the sky line for storms or fires which could be disaster to all the farmers in the area. She had a little garden that was growing very well, so that was another thing she must tend to. Besides Betty was demanding her attention.

That gave her an idea. She would visit Meg and ask her for help to look after Betty while she tended to the packing etc.

She walked over to Meg's with Betty tucked in a blanket, holding her in front. The baby soon nodded off during the half mile walk and even though Louise enjoyed the fresh air and the scents of the ripening grasses along the road, she was glad to reach her destination. As she got to Meg's, she saw her out with her chickens collecting eggs. She looked so much younger now that she let her hair hang down instead of in a bun.

"Hello, come on in and sit down. Here, I can put the baby on the bed, until she wakes up. She is such a lovely little thing,"

"I doubt that she will be there long. She is getting stronger every day,"

"Oh, the little mite, bless her,"

"I wanted to ask you for your help, just for a short time? We are moving into that house you vacated in town, after they do some work on it. I need to pack up household stuff and my garden need tending but Betty needs attention too,"

"Can I look after Betty?" Meg asked.

"It would surely help me out," answered Louise grinning. She could hear the enthusiasm in Meg's voice and knew what the answer would be.

"Of course, I would love too. How about if I bring her here for a day, would that help?"

"I would be very grateful," while Meg kept laughing and playing with the baby.

"That is what I wanted to hear. I was getting overwhelmed. And James is so busy!"

"We will work together with the harvest. John is also very busy getting ready for it. He wants to start building a barn, so that we can get a couple of cows, would you believe. I love it!" answered Meg.

"That is wonderful, perhaps James can help with that and I bet Bill would. He likes to build?"

"We will cross that bridge when we get there," said Meg as she poured a cup of tea for Louise when they heard another small voice.

"I had better run along before she gets hungry," said Louise hearing Betty crying.

"I can come tomorrow and collect Betty, that will give you a whole day," said Meg as she lifted Betty up from the bed where she had been sleeping and carried her around making her laugh.

"Betty, my darling, we must be going home, now," Louise mused as she wrapped the blanket around her back, bringing it to the front, cloistering the baby like a cocoon.

On the walk home, James met them half way on horseback. He stopped and motioned to Louise to give him Betty, saying, "Your first horseback ride, my little one,"

It was a relief to Louise, for even though she was just a baby, she was heavy.

"My goodness, thank you, James. She will love it."

At home after chores and supper dishes were washed and put away and Betty was bathed and fed and put to bed, they sat down to talk about the packing. Louise explained why she had walked over to Meg's which was to engage her help. She told him Meg offered to look after Betty for a whole day and that would give her time to pack properly she told him. James nodded in agreement and gave Louise a great big kiss. She could see he was tired and told him to go to bed she would be along, but there a few things she must do. Her washing was still on the line and she had more washing to do. She was also tired.

Louise continued to pack, but she had set her sights on harvesting her garden. She could do the canning in the evening, sew in the morning and pack in between. She was trying to use her time wisely. Harvest was coming up fast and she knew only too well, how busy they would be then. So much to do on so little time. Plus, as a force of habit, she continued to scan the horizon for smoke or storm clouds.

James was busy as well, getting the binder ready and making smudges for the horses. The mosquitos and flies were really thick this year. He carried a netting to put over his face. John had enlightened him about the smudges. John seemed to know a lot about farming and animals. James was also wanting to help John with his barn before winter set in, hoping that Bill would have time to come out and help both of them during harvest as well as finishing off the barn. The women had proved to be invaluable too and he was so glad he had Louise. Together, they would get through the fall.

Both were exhausted at night and went to sleep almost instantly. Of course, a little voice woke them up early, wanting attention. The morning sun was coming up in the east, welcoming everyone and you could hear the sound of horses and birds in the yard. It was such a glorious sound thought Louise as she was getting breakfast. She was looking forward to a day when she didn't have to watch Betty while she picked her peas or packed up a box of sewing supplies. Her projects would have to wait. However, she was determined to finish a dress for Betty's baptism hoping they would have a minister this fall. Every night they both prayed for help in that area.

Meg came to pick up Betty in a one horse buggy and was looking so perky and excited. Louise could tell she missed the children.

"I suppose you haven't heard anything from the children?" Louise asked as she put the kettle on. It was early and she was prepared for the day's work.

"I miss those children every day. They will write, once they are truly settled,"

"Well let's sit and have a cup of tea, Betty is snoozing right now. She was up very early this morning,"

"Louise, you look very tired? Are you feeling all right?"

"No more tired than last year, I feel,"

"Next time the Doctor comes, you should see him,"

"Perhaps a good idea. I am a little overwhelmed regarding the harvest and the move and all,"

"Let me help you, by looking after Betty. I love that little girl and she is growing like a weed. John is as bad as I am. He pays more attention to Betty than me sometimes, I swear."

To which laughter erupted and after a chat and some tea, Meg took care of Betty and left for home.

Louise sat for awhile and then decided to go to the garden and pick some peas and whatever else was ripening. It was a very warm day so she dug out her kerchief and put it on to protect her head and donned a light shirt to protect her arms deciding to make a smudge as well. She did not like the mosquitos. When she made her way to the garden she noted she was not alone. A doe was wandering through her garden helping herself to the peas.

"Shoo, get out of my garden," she hollered. The doe made a quick dash out of the garden and Louise realized she would have to watch her garden or loose it to the deer. She worked in the garden until she realized it was late afternoon. Oh my, she thought my little girl will be here before I know it so she headed to the house and began shelling peas, humming a little hymn while she did. It wasn't long before James came stumbling in declaring he had been stung and asking for something to put on them.

"Yes, I will make a soda paste to put on them," she answered. She hurried to apply it to his stings and worried about him when he sat down in the rocker and closed his eyes.

Oh, my man is so tired. We need to make this move. I am not the only one finding it difficult to keep up. A soda bath will help James and I want a bath as well. As she thought about it, she began preparations. As she worked, she glanced at James, often, not wanting to disturb him. He looked like he was asleep.

While outside, she gathered the clothes on the line, and picked up the tub she kept for bathing. It wasn't very big, but it had to do. As she mused about bathing, she saw Meg coming down the road bringing Betty back. Meg was laughing at the baby, as she handed her down to Louise, saying, "We have the most glorious day. The bees are really bad right now, but believe it or not we did not get stung."

"That is good. James, however did more than once,"

"Is he okay?"

"Yes, I believe so, he is asleep in the rocker right now, but I can assure you that Betty will wake him up,"

"She is a marvel, that girl. I thank you for letting me look after her and I can do that again if you want me to,"

"I really would appreciate that. I have so many things to do, and time is of the essence right now."

"Just let me know and by the way Bill showed up today to help with the barn. What a surprise. He also said your house is looking better too."

"That is great! James will be so glad,"

"See you soon, Louise. Come over anytime," she said as she waved and drove off.

Quickly Louise, took Betty inside, and James of course, woke up with a start and smiling said, "Oh, here's my little beauty," as he stretched his arms out toward the baby. She smiled at him and nestled on his lap, reaching for his face. Louise smiled as she watched the two of them. She noted the stings didn't seem to bother him.

In the next few days, James joined the barn building team at John's until he decided it was time to cut the crop continually watching the horizon. They worked steady, each in his own thoughts, complimenting each other while hammering the boards into place. They knew it will not be complete by harvest but if they had a two-day neighborhood work bee it would be close. John would be able to finish it when he had the time.

All the while, Louise was kept busy. She was doing an amazing job with Betty and canning and packing and trying to sew a little as well. James was in awe of her talents but worried that it may be getting too much. People were forever calling in to ask her to sew something and she never could say no. They must get to town soon for her sake. He was hoping to talk to Meg for more help with the baby. The two of them were so tired and seemed to take two steps forward and one back.

During the next few days, James noted that Louise seemed to be slowing down and frequently wore a frown. When he asked about it, she shrugged and said she was fine, but he was beginning to worry. He would ask Bill when they were building to find out when the doctor was going to be in town and he would take time to go with Louise or he would ask Meg to go with her to see the doctor.

James continued to help with barn building and made his way over to John's by horseback. It was a beautiful clear day, with nary a cloud in the sky. It awed him to see the sky so blue and the grain so yellow. How lucky he felt although a black cloud followed him around lately regarding Louise. He wasn't going to take a chance there. He couldn't wait until they moved. Perhaps then, the daily chores wouldn't be so hard and he felt she was lonely as well. She never seemed to have time to visit. Meg had put him wise to that and with a baby to tend as well.

When he got to John's, he noted the men were resting at the moment. He would stay and help for a while. He waved to them as he dismounted and walked beside the horse to the workers. There were at least five working today and the barn was looking pretty good. The sides were all up and it looked like they were beginning on the roof. Another couple of days and it will be almost done, just in time too, he thought with the crop ripening steadily.

"Hello, looks like the barn is coming along?"

John laughed and answered him saying, "Just about and in good time too,"

"Is Meg around?" James asked before he tied up his horse.

"Yes, inside the house, I believe," hollering that James was there.

James went to the door, just as Meg came out.

"What is it James, is Louise okay?" she sounded worried rushing towards him.

"As far as I know, she is fine, however, do you know when the doctor will be in by any chance. I would like her to see him. She is so tired and wears a frown sometimes when she thinks I am not looking. She looks pale to me, you know, her complexion has been so healthy looking,"

"You know, James, I am going in tomorrow to help the doctor by chance. Could I take her in with me and perhaps you could pick her up later? I will have to stay a day or so, while the doctor is there."

"That would work for me. I am going to stay and help for a little while on the barn,"

"I will go and see Louise, James. It will give me a chance to chat with her. Can I use your horse?"

"Why yes, she could do with some exercise,"

Meg ran back inside and came sailing out, grabbing the horses reins and within minutes was racing down the road.

"What a girl?"

"Yes, she is one in a million," replied John as he stopped momentarily and watched her hair flying as she galloped down the road, then, nailed the last nail in the frame for the roof.

The time had come for the men to hoist the roof frame up onto its place. The men, sweaty and dusty, stood and studied it for a time, discussing different ways to do this. It was John that decided how to do the job and organized the men. It took some heaving and levering to get it into place, but when they did a great whoop went up with the men.

"When the crop is in, we are going to have a barn dance here," stated John excitedly.

Upon which a great deal of excitement was felt among the men, who cheered John on as he danced around the building. James was amused by all the excitement even though he was not a dancing type of person. His ideology was strictly the spiritual side of life and living. However, he would not object to this news at all. He knew the news of the barn dance would soon get around and almost everyone would be in favor. It would bring all the neighbors together and create some excitement which they so desperately needed.

While this was going on, Meg was at Louise' and noticed immediately when she saw her that things were not quite right.

"Louise what in the world is wrong. You look terrible," she cried quickly dropping the reins of the horse.

"Just had a little upset tummy," replied Louise.

When Meg looked at her face, she suddenly realized what was wrong and asked her, if she was in family way, at which Louise made a face. "That's all I need right now, with the harvest and move and Betty and all," she replied and started to cry.

On hearing the noise, Betty woke up from her nap and demanded attention.

"She probably needs changing and the diapers are on the line. They should be dry by now. I can't seem to keep up with everything, the garden, the packing, the washing, and to boot I don't feel like eating and the smell of meat cooking just turns my stomach. I just don't want James to worry at this time. He needs all the help he can get. That's why I haven't told him," she answered sporadically.

"Louise, he knows something is wrong. That's why I am here. He wants me to accompany you to the doctor as soon as possible," said Meg trying to sooth Louise' nerves.

"Oh, I have been trying so hard, to keep it from him, but he did say something to that effect this morning. I went outside because I was throwing up. He must have heard me," Louise said with some reservation.

"Now, tomorrow, I believe the doctor will be in town, and I usually help him with his patients. Why don't you and I and Betty, go to town in the morning. You can stay at Liz's while I look after Betty and the doctor's patients."

"How can you do both?" demanded Louise.

"It gives me something to do, between the appointments and a baby almost always makes people smile which I believe makes them feel better for a little while,"

"Okay," Louise sighed going to look after Betty, however Meg beat her to it and Betty was just gurgling away. Louise, gathered the clothes off the line while Meg played with the baby. It was a relief now that the secret was out. She would tell James tonight. Why is it that everything comes at once?

"By the way, Louise, John is planning a barn dance at the end of harvest. I will need help with the food etc."

"But Meg, James is not one for dances. He would never promote it,"

"Whether or not he does, the neighbors are all in favor and it will happen,"

"I can help with the preparation maybe, but we will only be there at the beginning and then I know, we will leave. Maybe it is time for some social gathering," Louise mused.

"Well, we will have it and I look forward to visiting. You can come at the beginning and when the music starts well?" Meg knew only too well, how religious James was and felt that Louise was raised that way too. She had no idea what a dance was because they did not stay the day they got married to watch the people, hear the music and feel the excitement that caused the people to dance in the street. Adding, "I must get home, but I will be here bright and early in the morning."

"Thank you, Meg. We will be ready," Louise answered, closing her eyes in relief, now that it was out. She was sure Meg would say something to James, but he would pretend not to know.

Louise finished her chores and then concentrated on Betty, getting her bathed and fed. She sat down in her rocker to feed her and both fell asleep. That's how James found them when he returned. Smiling at the sight, he gently lifted Betty up and put her in her crib. He kissed her gently, covering her little body. When he turned, Louise woke up startled, her hair falling out of its bun and mumbling something James could not understand.

"You are so tired, my dear, why don't you just go to bed? I will make out just fine. Meg has fed us so all I need now is a wash, a cup of tea, and I will be right behind you,"

It didn't take long for Louise to get ready for bed. She was indeed tired, Then, she remembered the baby and looked around wildly. James set her at ease pointing to the crib where she lay fast asleep.

"Thank you!' Louise answered wearily, heading for bed.

Both were tired and slept soundly. Even the howling of the coyotes didn't wake them, but the baby did, all too soon.

Louise, slowly dressed and picked her up. She would let James have another few winks. She sat for a moment, then looked out the window, holding Betty. Betty, however, wasn't interested in looking out the window, she wanted her breakfast and now.

"Okay, little one. I will get your bottle ready. We will have to wake your Daddy now too. Yes, and Aunty Meg will be here soon as well," she murmured as she touched James shoulder. He woke up with a start, realizing Louise was already up and dressed. Hearing Betty, he smiled and rose, calling her name. He liked this time of day with his little family. They were his pride and joy.

"Meg will be here soon, to take us to town. So if you will hold Betty for me, I will get breakfast. It looks like it might rain. Clouds are gathering in the west."

"All right, my dear, give me my little one, I can feed her while you do that,"

Betty finished her bottle and contentedly sat on father's knee watching her mother working around the stove. He gave her a ride on his knee which made her giggle. It made them both laugh as they sat down to eat.

"James, before I go, I must tell you something. I believe that I am with child again."

"Well, I am delighted, but you must slow down and rest more,"

"We will know more today. I need something to gain my appetite back and I constantly throw up, which is not good,"

"I am glad you are going to the Doctor, today. Don't worry everything will work out," James said with emphasis.

Louise was relieved now it was out in the open. It would be good to go to town anyway, just to see Liz and visit with the two. It has been too long.

It wasn't long before Meg was at the door with her horse and buggy. Louise hurried to get ready, while James played with Betty.

"Come, Betty, we must not keep Aunty Meg waiting," James kissed them both waving goodbye and watching them drive away. He stood there until they were out of sight. *Just as I thought, she is with child and she is going through the same problems as before. I do pray that she will be okay. I don't know what I would do, if I lost her. She is such a rock! I thank God everyday for bringing her here.* Shaking his head as if to clear his mind, he started to clear the table of the breakfast dishes first, and then realized he better get to work. As he glanced out the window, he noted some black clouds in the South.

"Oh, looks like we are in for some rain," he muttered to himself and hurried outside to ride over to John's. He was going to give him one more day on the barn. He pursed his lips, thinking about the barn, while he talked to the horses. He was going to ride over on one, but decided to take the buggy and use both horses. They needed the exercise. Before he left though, he grabbed his hat and raincoat. As he hurried out the door again a barrage of insects met him. He realized what they were and worried knowing that Louise wasn't going to like it.

Meg and Louise and the baby arrived at Liz's within the hour. It started to blow, so they let the horses run. Louise wasn't worried about the rain but those green looking things that were buzzing all over the place. The horses snorted constantly because of them.

"Meg, what are those bugs? Where in the world did they come from?"

"They are grasshoppers, Louise. They won't hurt you, but they are annoying. John was saying he was glad there weren't so many otherwise we would lose the crop. They would eat everything in sight."

"Another thing I have to learn? Is there never an end?" Louise uttered sounding despondent. She liked this time of year, the smells of ripening grasses and berries and the golden appearance

of the grain, it always reminded her of a good harvest and an end
to all the hard work getting the grain to that stage. There is so
much to this country and now I understand why James said to be
brave.

A misty rain started just as they arrived as Liz met them at the
door and taking Betty, rushed inside, with Louise right behind.
Meg carried on to the stables hollering she would be right back.

"I am so glad to see you both, and my how this little one is
growing. It is hard to believe?" gushed Liz.

"I am glad to be here as well. It had been too long, but farm
work never ends, and now those pesky grasshoppers," replied
Louise.

"The doctor hasn't arrived yet, so I will put the kettle on. Sit
and relax and I will join you," said Liz.

"Thank you, I will have to change Betty first, before she starts
putting up a fuss," said Louise with a grin.

"Were you going to see the doctor?" asked Liz.

"Yes, I believe I am with child, well I know that I am. I can't
keep any food down,"

"Goodness, the same as the last time?"

"Seems like it,"

"Hello, you two, the doctor hasn't arrived yet, so I can chat
for a while," called Meg as she plumped herself down in the first
available chair.

They chatted amicably about a lot of things. Louise was
starved for visits with other women. There were so many questions
she wanted to ask. She told them that once in a while the neighborhood women would drop over, but she did not know them as
well.

"Oh, Louise, there is a letter here for you. The Post Master called me about it. Yes, we now have a post office. He hoped soon they would have mail delivered to the farms. Oh and we are going to have a saloon, and rooming house and I believe there are plans for a dance hall, although not right away. There have been men asking around and I do need some help, maybe there will even be another café or diner. People are coming in every day. It is keeping us so busy and Bill wants to work the harvest. I might have to hire a girl for a little while. This place is booming, I tell you," said Liz.

"I wondered at the amount of people around and what they were building here. I am glad of a post office. I will have to go and get my letter, I hope it is from my parents," she said excitedly.

"Meg what have you been up to. You look so healthy and happy. It's wonderful!"

"I am happy, John is the best man I could have ever wished for. We are praying for a decent crop and hoping those bugs don't eat it all," answered Meg.

"They come every year, I think," replied Liz.

"I believe, like John says, a few is okay, but when hoards of them are seen on the skyline, that's when we worry. The farmers say, you can see them coming for miles. They can be so thick they blot out the sun, would you believe," added Meg.

"I have heard stories about their attack. They leave nothing behind, no grass, gardens, crops etc."

"I have said two prayers," said Louise at which they all laughed.

"Good for you, Louise," said Liz as the Doctor entered through the misty rain and called to Meg to come to the office along with Louise. Louise followed Meg but left Betty behind with Liz, promising not to be long.

"We will be just fine. I have no customers right now and I need the time to rest and play with her,"

The visit to the doctor confirmed everything. He listened to her and then prescribed a tonic to help with her appetite. It will be the same again, I must insist that you rest a lot.

"We are moving into town, so I should be able to do just that. The harvest will be over and James is taking over the management of the stables here,"

"Good, then I want to see you again in a month. I also want to see that young lady I have been hearing about,"

"She is doing just fine, growing like a weed. She will be crawling soon I feel," suddenly realizing that Betty was at Liz's, she stopped talking immediately and prepared to get going.

"See you next month, Louise," replied the Doctor, as he turned to Meg for another patient.

Louise was at Liz's in a flash, only to find the Liz talking to the baby contentedly. Liz was totally absorbed in the little girl and didn't even hear Louise come in.

"Looks like you two have been having a good time?"

"We have, we got along quite well, thank you,"

"That's good, I am okay the Doctor said and gave me some medicine for the appetite and throwing up,"

"Did he tell you to take it easy?"

"That too,"

"Good and you should, especially now at harvest. The neighbor women will help, but you have to tell them. You shouldn't be ashamed of that. We help each other in this wild west country."

"I promise to do just that. I just wanted to be sure, first of all," Louise admitted.

"Now, how about a cup of tea and a little leisure. I will tell you all about what is happening here," Liz said with a grin.

"People are coming into Lashburn steady. The rails and the Red River carts are kept busy bringing in supplies. The General Store is so busy; he has had to hire another person. The Mounted police are here every day helping, organizing and generally advising people where to go and what to do. I have people asking me every day about supplies or tents or whatever they can do. I feed some very hungry people with children every day for nothing. I don't know how long I can do that. I hate to see someone go hungry, especially little children,"

"You are doing God's work, Liz. I hope when we move into town that I can be of help. Right now harvesting is upon us and I know that I will be busy for a couple of months with that. Plus, I am carrying an extra load this fall and looking after Betty. I will be relying on the neighbor women this year especially,"

"I can't wait until you join us in town. It will be so nice to have someone to visit with, and Bill is looking forward to it too. He wants to help build the church, you know. He is quite keen on it. We noticed too, quite a lot of people are showing up at the school house for Sunday service. James has done so well keeping the services going but I am sure he could use some help."

Soon Meg was at the door. Louise asked for a moment. She wanted to know if there was an Eaton's catalog around, but before she finished the sentence, Liz handed her one to take with her.

"Your buggy awaits, my ladies," Meg said with a grin.

"We will be right with you, my Lord," answered Louise with a grin also.

The women laughed and Betty joined in as if she knew all along what was going on. It made the three women laugh even louder and longer.

"Take care, you two. I miss you both," cried Liz as she lifted Betty up to Louise, who was already in the buggy with Meg.

"Bye for now," said Louise holding Betty's hand up to wave as well.

The air was warm. The misty rain had quit and left a fresh sweet smell behind. Meg and Louise savored the air as they drove along. It was a perfect evening driving home and soon Betty was sleeping peacefully.

"I think Betty is worn out. Maybe she will sleep in tomorrow, although I doubt it. As soon as James moves in the morning, she is smiling and mumbling at him and he can't resist picking her up."

"That's wonderful, Louise."

As they saunter along, they met a couple of wagons, coming towards them and two following them.

"I wonder where they are going?" sighed Meg. "And where are they coming from?"

"This country will be overrun soon, if this keeps up. The land all around us has been purchased, I know. Ours will be up for sale this fall as well. But first we must get the crop off. That also means that I will be in great demand with the binders. Word does travel far and wide you know," commented Louise.

"Your efficiency on the sewing machine as been duly noted, my dear," answered Meg as she pulled up to Louise' home.

"Thank you Meg, you are a dear. We will be over to see you soon,"

"You are always welcome. Come some evening before the men really get busy, and we will have a proper chat. Especially now that your news is out."

"We will," said Louise as she handed Betty down to James, who was waiting for them at the door. Betty immediately woke up and waving her hands, smiled at her father, who was calling her.

"You were waiting for the confirmation, weren't you?" laughed Louise.

"Umm," he nodded smiling.

"It's confirmed, and I am healthy, the Doctor says, just take more rests during the day," said Louise smiling.

"Okay, and I am going to make sure of that. I will help with Betty as well, since she is growing."

"I am weary now. How would you like to feed and bath your little girl, tonight?"

"Absolutely, my pleasure. My hands are a bit rough though. Do you think she will mind?"

"I don't think she will even notice,"

"Then to bed with you. See you in the morning," he said lifting Betty up high in the air amid lots of happy mumblings.

Louise fell asleep as soon as she laid down. Betty awoke her with cries as the sun came up, and she arose slowly wondering what time it was.

"You have slept the whole night, my dear," murmured James as he went to get Betty from her crib, before she started a full-scale cry.

"I have?"

She dressed quickly and proceeded to start breakfast, while James entertained the baby. She will be wanting her breakfast as well, she thought. She noted, however, that James frowned when he looked out the window.

"Are worried about me or something else?" she asked.

"I am truly concerned about those grasshoppers. They could damage our crop, to a point where it will be worthless. John and I were talking about it yesterday. We would like to visit some of the other farmers, to see what they have found out or know, today. John also explained that he heard of a new kind of wheat that has been developed for this country that is high yielding and early maturing. He is looking to put some in next spring."

"Do you suppose the weather has something to do with those bugs?" she asked as she poured their porridge and gave Betty her bottle. Smiling James saw that Betty was already trying to hold her bottle and gurgling. He shook his head when it landed on the floor. Picking it up, he laughed out loud putting it on the table, continuing to look outside.

"Off you go then, we have work to do, my good man, and find out all you can about those pesky things. I dislike what they do to my washing?"

With that he left the house, and she could hear the horses whinnying as he neared. They were ready for a run.

Louise finished the breakfast dishes and began to wash out Betty's diapers. The wind had picked up so it was a good time to get them on the clothes line to dry. Louise looked wistfully at the clothes line. She couldn't take Betty out with her because of those bugs so she would have to wait until she had her nap before hanging the washing out and I need to check out the garden.

The garden was not in very good shape. Some of the leaves had been chewed off making the stems bare. "Oh my we do have a problem here," murmured Louise.

She walked around the yard, first checking the garden and then walked out to the field to have a look. She counted the grasshoppers hopping about, wondering at the nature of the insect. Louise caught one and put it in her hankie to keep and have a good look at it. She would show it to James.

Louise checked the washing on the line for insects. She had had to rewash the last bunch and did not relish doing it again. She had just finished when James came driving in. Why he is home early, she thought. I wonder why?

"You are home early, what is up?" she called as he unhooked the horses and tied them up.

"John and I are going to Lashburn tonight, to see if we can find someone that knows about these pesky things,"

"Makes sense, but is there someone in town that can help?"

"John believes there is a government office in Saskatoon and perhaps they can help,"

"We want to arrange a meeting of the farmers, to help combat this pest," replied James.

"Will you be announcing that information at the Sunday service?" asked Louise

"That is my plan, I also want to find out if there is any news from the Church of England as to whether we are getting a minister or not?"

"Good, plan," said Louise as she attended to Betty's supper as James finished his as John knocked at the door and asked if James was ready.

"Off you two go, we are fine here," said Louise as she ushered them out the door.

It would be a time, after Betty was in bed, to do some of her tatting. The lace would some in handy in future projects. As she went about her chores, washing up and getting the baby ready for bed, she thought about their future, hoping that they would be able to live a little more comfortably in town. Soon she was rocking Betty to sleep. Sometimes she felt herself nodding off. It was peaceful right now. After snoozing for a bit, she decided that Betty should be in her crib and proceeded to do just that. Sitting back in her rocker, she picked up her lace work, and worked at it until she started to nod off again. Putting her work aside, she rested her head, and immediately fell fast asleep. Only to be jolted awake by the door opening.

"Oh, my," she murmured, "I must have fallen asleep," to James who remarked while taking his coat off.

"You will not believe what I just heard?" he said excitedly. Louise looked at him questioningly.

"What?"

"We have a minister and his wife coming in about three weeks and they are staying at Liz's, until they decide what to do. And the government is sending someone out to help us decide what to do with the grasshopper situation. I will have to announce that this Sunday at our service. I am so happy," he danced around Louise, still sitting. "How about some tea, my love," but realized how tired Louise was decided to make it himself.

Smiling Louise remained in her rocker, thinking how lucky they were.

Chapter Thirteen

Harvest

Harvesting continued and Louise and James made headway in their move to town. Both were satisfied with the bindering, and the following threshing. They had help from the neighbors, but Louise was still feeling very tired. They prayed every morning and night for assistance and never forgot to give thanks. The pesky grasshoppers had somehow lessoned, except for the odd one hanging around. The mosquitos were still a nuisance.

During the next few weeks, their furniture and horses would be moved. James registered his land for sale and found it was soon swallowed up. People were coming in regularly looking for land and this one was highly regarded because there was a house on the property.

Soon James, Louise and Betty were ensconced in their new house and welcomed some peace and quiet. What they hadn't realized was the change around town with new businesses being established right and left. There was an immediate need for living quarters and if they got a new minister where would he live?

The discussion came up the next time Louise went to see Liz and offer some help.

Liz, however, did not want Louise to do extra work due to her condition. They talked at length, when Liz offered a temporary solution. Betty in the meantime was fast asleep on Louise' knee.

Liz said they could stay there for a short time. I could even give them room and board for half of what I usually charge, if it would help which was a relief to Louise.

"They should be arriving soon, how I don't know, just that they are on their way," replied Louise.

"Good let's just wait and see, shall we? And give me that baby of yours for a couple of hours, so I can spoil her," asked Liz, noting that Betty was beginning to wake up.

"I sure can. I know I could use the time to do some unpacking and sorting. I have some sewing that needs doing as well. James is over at the stables, checking on supplies and probably won't be home until supper, so that would give me some time, thank you!"

After depositing Betty on Liz's knee, Louise left in a hurry. She knew just what had to be done and couldn't wait to get to it. Besides she had to decide what to make for supper as well. As she hurried, she prayed for this good time and the future minister and his wife. She hoped that this would solve the problem for the time being. Before she arrived home, however, a team of horses stopped beside her and asked for James. She looked at them questioningly, and the gentleman, quickly informed her that he was the new minister and this was his wife.

"Oh my, you're here! My husband is James and he is at the stables now. You might take your horse over there. It is just down the road a way," she answered stuttering.

She forgot to introduce herself. It caught her completely by surprise. Turning around she hurried back to Liz's. Liz saw her coming and was at the door, wondering what in the world was wrong.

"Is something wrong, Louise?" she asked.

"The mmminister and his wife are here," she said breathlessly.

"Okay, send them to me. We will sort this out."

She collected Betty and turned to go, but James was calling her and walking toward her with the newcomers.

"This is my wife, Louise,' he said as he approached her.

"We already met, I am Rev. Jones, and this is my wife, Anna"

"It's good to meet you, and this is Betty," said Louise as she nodded towards the baby.

"James, Liz has indicated that she may be able to help in regards to living quarters until we find something suitable,"

"That is a good idea. It will give you a chance to get to know the people and the land. Have you been here long?"

The minister, stated that they had only arrived in Halifax, when a call came through to travel to Western Canada where a minister was desperately needed. He was a thin man, with a long nose above a bushy beard. His clothes were immaculate. His wife who was of small build, with long black hair that hung down in curls around a lovely complexion and perfect shaped lips but no smile.

"Then this will give you some time to get acquainted. Let's go and meet Liz, the owner of the rooming house,"

Mrs. Jones, didn't seem too impressed never uttering a word. She looked askance at her husband several times, as if this was not her decision and liking. He, however was enthusiastic and completely ignored his wife.

James introduced the minister and his wife to Liz. Telling them that this was the best place for them at this time and leaving them to settle in.

"Thank you, we will need all the help we can get. I am afraid that we don't know very much about this country at all," Rev. Jones said as his wife hovered in the background.

Liz addressed Mrs. Jones, "Why don't you settle in. I will show you your room and then if you would like something to eat, well, I will see to that," getting a nod of agreement from the Reverent but not from his wife.

After settling in and while his wife was resting, the minister asked Liz if by chance they could pay for their room and board by working for her because they didn't have much money. Liz was caught off guard. She told him they could work something out. There was not much for him, but his wife could help in the diner when it gets busy. The reverend seemed pleased about it.

Liz wondered about these two. As for his wife, she hadn't really got to know her at all. Could she really look after the tables and patrons? We'll see how things go, I guess. As Louise would say, 'If it's God's will'.

Two days later, Liz came running over to Louise.

"You got to help me," she burst out.

"That woman will kill all my business and believe it or not, I don't know what to do with them,"

"What does she do?" asked Louise.

"She is preaching the Bible to everyone that comes through that door, and I have to keep reminding her to set the table or clean it and wash the dishes. She just looks at me like I am an idiot and walks away. Nothing gets done properly,"

"I will tell James to come over, as soon as he is free. Maybe he should talk to both of them. Sit down, and have a cup of tea with me."

"Thank you, I am at my wits end. People are walking out as soon as she starts preaching. My business will go down. I can't wait until Bill comes back. He is still helping John. They should be finished soon," Liz said all in one breath, as she sat down.

Louise did not know what to think. They had been so excited at getting a minister at last. She handed Liz a cup of tea, pursing her lips.

"I think we need James to deal with this," answered Louise.

"Thanks, Louise, I feel so down. Winter will soon be here and I don't think they have any idea at all about clothes or living quarters and the people who are from different cultural and spiritual backgrounds," Liz said agitated.

Betty decided that she should be heard then and that cheered Liz up immensely.

"Oh, my, the little lady wants attention and that is what she will get," said Liz as she marched into the bedroom and picked up a smiling Betty out of her crib.

The tenseness in the room was immediately calmed and attention was diverted for the time being. Soon they would be routed back to reality and problems. When she left, Louise promised to send James over as soon as possible.

James was jubilant as he came through the door, but one look at Louise' frowning face, stopped him, "What in the world is wrong?"

"You need to go over to Liz, immediately, she is having all sorts of problems with the new minister and his wife, especially his wife. She is afraid, she will lose all her patrons, if she continues to stay there. She preaches, as Liz calls it, to everyone that comes through the door whether they want it or not and most just turn around and leave. Also her so-called job is definitely lacking. Helping in the diner, seems to be beneath her. I have never seen Liz so worked up," explained Louise as she sat Betty in her chair.

James, immediately turned around without taking off his coat and hurried over to see Liz, vowing to get to the bottom of it. He had been so looking forward to the Sunday sermon by this fellow.

James took one look at Liz and knew that things were not good. She looked haggard and unusually cryptic when he greeted her. The situation was indeed tense.

"Is the reverend and his wife here?" he asked

"They went for a walk, and it is a good thing, because I was ready to blow up. They don't seem to get it. She does not like taking orders and leaves everything for me to do. Like they are staying here free and have a right to," Liz was steamed to be sure.

"I will wait for them and try to get through to them that you are doing them a favor and they are definitely taking advantage of you," answered James.

It was a while before they returned and seemed to be jubilant. When he saw James, he grew excited.

"We saw the school house, where you said they hold the Sunday services. My wife thought she would like to go during school time and speak to the children," he said with a little scepticism.

"First of all, you have not been hired as a minister, yet. I also noted that you are both taking advantage of this rooming house. If you do not comply with the decision to give you free room and board for work, then you will have to start paying or move on. I have yet to see any papers from you or actually any information. I suggest that you cover the Sunday service and let the people decide whether or not you are welcome here."

James was adamant. He did not like the idea of people taking advantage of Liz's generosity and wondered what they really thought they were doing. Rev. Jones replied that he was sorry, it had gotten out of hand.

"I really wanted to work among the natives in this country," said Mrs. Jones, ignoring everything James had explained.

"Then, I believe you are going to be disappointed. The natives here are not that friendly, and often create havoc amongst the farmers,"

"But they can be taught?" she countered.

"Well, maybe you should go out to the reserve and see for yourself," James suggested. At which she became overjoyed. Continuing after that he added, "In the meantime, I suggest that you get to work and do what you were supposed to do in order to stay here. May I suggest sir, you talk to your wife or you will be asked to leave."

He motioned to Liz to meet him outside and told her that he had given them an ultimatum and if they do not do any work for you, you can ask them to leave and let them find a place themselves. No more help!

"Thank you, I am hoping Bill will be back tonight and I know he will not put up with this nonsense." Liz said as she waved good bye.

Sunday, found the minister and his wife without room and board. Liz had officially, decided enough was enough and she was losing business left and right. She wished them well, but was decidedly glad to see the back of them.

They did show up for the Sunday service however and took charge immediately, moving the desks around to suit themselves. People started coming in just before twelve and were wondering at the changes. The minister and his wife were not at the door to greet the people but kept on working at the front of the school. Finally, when James and Louise came in, they did stop and look for approval. James however, calmly suggested that they begin the service, for people were coming in steady by this time.

Rev. Jones started the service off with a bang on the teacher's desk. He introduced himself and his wife, who shared the podium with him raising eyebrows. They both got right into the sermon, which began by denouncing Satan and all his ways, then in a fire and brimstone speech declared each and every sinner to change their ways and start listening to God's word and to start praying a lot. He said they needed cleansing and saving from their nefarious ways. It was not pleasant. Mrs. Jones interjected frequently with 'amen' or "thank you, God."

Finally, one of the burly farmers rose, along with his family and left quite noisily. In a few minutes another family left. Rev. Jones did not seem to notice this action until he looked up and only James, Louise and Betty remained in the room. He looked surprised and disheartened. His wife suddenly declared that this area certainly needed a lot of work plus they don't even dress properly.

James spoke up at that point saying, " The people here are honest, hard working people who have spoken. You, my friend, will have to find another church. The Saloon has rooms upstairs and will put you up for the night for a fee and you will have to find your own transportation to perhaps Saskatoon, which I pray will be better for you."

Louise, in the meantime, while looking after Betty, had been sitting beside Liz and Bill, who had left soon after it started. They would go over and let them know what James had told them. As they made their way over to Liz's, another buggy arrived and was sitting out front.

"Excuse me," he called, "I am looking for a James Whiteley, regarding a ministerial job?"

"I am James, and who may I ask are you?"

"I received a letter from Rev. Lloyd regarding a problem in this area. Sorry my name is Evans, Reverend Evans and this is my wife, Lorette, at your service," he said amiably.

"Come along then, tie up your horse and join us for a cup of tea,"

Soon they were all sitting in Liz's dining area. Both new-comers were jovial and quite pleasant to talk to. Mrs. Evans spoke to Louise and Betty and looking up at Liz and said, "This is such a lovely place, you are to be commended, I thank you for the tea and scones, and please let us pay you for it." She was of medium build, with a pleasant face and dark hair tied in a bun at the nape. She showed lovely dimples when she smiled and beautiful teeth and there was no sign of makeup. Her dress was the same as Louise' long ankle length, with sleeves that extended to her wrists and a high lace neckline.

"I am so glad you liked it, please let it be my gift," admitted Liz, pleased.

James continued to explain to the new minister, what had just transpired at the school house and that he would have to go back and rearrange the tables for school the next day. He expressed the fact that the people were not happy with the type of sermon he was preaching and that they all left, some noisily and some quietly."

"Oh, dear, there will be a lot of confidence building to be done, I fear," the minister answered adding, "if you want us to stay, we must visit the farmers and get their trust back. He was of medium, slim build. His hair was short and dark with some gray showing at the sides. His voice was melodic. He explained that his wife would be helpful with people, but works only in the background.

"I am willing to give it a try. We will take you out to a couple of farms tomorrow," decided James, when he saw that Louise was nodding her approval. "I will have to get someone to take my place at the stables for the day, first. Where will you stay?"

"If Mrs. Long will have us, I would appreciate a bed here," he answered.

Liz nodded agreement and told them that a bedroom was indeed ready for occupancy and told them they could put their bags there now. She never mentioned cost, just yet, wondering if they were going to pay. Before they were escorted to the bedroom, the minister, asked her whether she wanted pay now or later?

"You can pay me later, perhaps you might need more than a day or two,"

"That's settled, then. Now James let me help you with the school house. It will give me a chance to look around and get a feel for the area. This is new territory for me. And my wife, would probably like a rest now. It has been a long day."

"Let's go then, bring your horse & buggy to the stable first, then we will go to the school house."

Louise, was ready for a rest as well, and Betty had fallen asleep as they talked. She was getting to be almost too heavy for her to carry, so she handed her to James and they made to leave. As they walked home, James remarked how different this man and woman were. They were so willing to step in and help and never asking for any. Let's pray this works out. I am afraid it is too much for me to keep serving in that capacity.

The reverend said that there are a lot of missionaries coming from all over. He talked to more men and woman bound not only to save the world but to inspire and convert the natives and they had no idea of where they were going. They were strange bedfellows. At home, James laid Betty to rest and suggested Louise do so as well. He thought she looked extremely tired today.

On his way to the stable, the minister brought his horse and buggy and got busy unhitching the horse. He seemed to be adept at doing this and also very spry and willing which James noted.

The visit to the farms the next day was extremely good. Rev. Evans got along with everyone and enjoyed talking about the farms and farming, wanting to know everything which the farmers were only too willing to relate. He was also interested in the families all around and asked about their children and their background, which pleased so many. They told James how much they liked him and were willing to take another chance on the Sunday service.

James was overjoyed and gave thanks quietly on the way home. When he stopped at Liz's, Lorette was washing dishes in the kitchen and chatting away. Liz looked like she was visibly enjoying the camaraderie.

When James got home, he found Louise in a lot of pain, but still trying to deal with Betty. "Louise, you must go and lie down. What is the matter?"

"I just don't feel very good. Maybe nerves are all," she answered.

"You need to rest more, and I believe we must get you some help with Betty. She is getting much too big to be carried around. I will ask around, there are people coming all the time and a lot of them have girls that might like a little job, to make some money,"

"We can't afford much," answered Louise.

"Whatever, it is, I believe it is necessary in your condition," said James, his brow furrowed in worry.

Sunday came and Rev. Evans served the people close to what James had been doing, pleasing the people immensely. They sang, Lorette played the piano, and they laughed at some of his sayings and thoroughly enjoyed his sermon which included passages from the Bible, but was more like he was talking to each and everyone of them.

"Thank you, Rev. Evans, you have made many friends today and no one left, I noted," said James shaking his hand. He nodded to Mrs. Evans as well, as she too had made friends and who helped Louise with Betty. She actually gathered the children and told them a delightful story about Jesus. All of them sitting so quiet and listening except Betty who crawled around the whole time. It didn't seem to matter to Lorette, she just smiled and continued talking. The parents watched as the children listened to every word.

Afterwards Louise, wondered, was it her voice that caught the children's attention. She seemed to have a way with young people and that was wonderful and needed here. She told James that this couple was going to fit in like a glove and she was glad.

"They will be just fine, I declare and furthermore I don't think we need to worry about them, they seem to have it all in hand, sort of," James added.

"Today, I am going to take it easy and rest while Betty has hers," admitted Louise.

"The pressure is off, now, and I am still going to look for some help for you," uttered James, while he played with the baby or little lady, as he called her. Adding, he said, "today is the Lord's day and we will honor it," as he yawned.

They would enjoy the day together. The fall had taken its toll on Louise and she desperately needed some time with James and their baby.

After Sunday, everything went smoothly. Meg and John came in to see them with plans for future development. They were happy to see them and hear the latest. Meg drew Louise aside and told her that she suspected she was with child and was so excited but so nervous about it. Louise was overcome with excitement and calmed her by saying, "I am sure you will have no trouble and I will pray for that. We can pray together, besides now I have an excuse to sew two smocks," after which Meg smiled and they went back to the men, arm in arm. Meg knew how Louise felt about prayer and often saw her close her eyes and drop her head in prayer mode during the time they spent together.

The four of them, oops five of them had a great chat and Louise, of course, served her famous scones with jam. It was a happy reunion. As they were having their tea, Liz and Bill joined them. Both were jovial and the afternoon was light hearted. Liz guessed about Meg, immediately, like she had a second sense. At first, she looked concerned, but Louise put her at ease and soon they were talking and laughing. Meg wanted to know all that was going on in town and the newest buildings and businesses. It was like old times for these six. So many changes were happening. Louise informed them that a shoe and clothing store was coming, and a hair salon, so she would not be so busy that way and it would be a blessing because she would have more time with her children.

Bill and Liz expressed their delight in the new minister and his wife. They were only too helpful in every way and made sure they paid their way. It was so nice for a change.

"I will allow them to stay as long as they like. However, knowing them they will make their own way, I am sure." Liz said with a grin.

Towards the end of the afternoon, Meg and John had to leave, but vowed to get together at least once a month, if possible. Meg invited them all out to the farm, before winter settled in for good.

Baby Florence Arrives

A month later, winter did set in for good. The wind blew and blew, piling the snow up against the house, covering the front steps, and surrounding paths, including the path to the outhouse. No one was moving unless absolutely necessary. James had very little business at the stables, so he came home to help Louise. She was looking very tired, he thought, and worried that this time her condition was taking its toll.

Before he went home, however, he checked on Liz and Bill, making sure they were okay, and asking Liz if she knew of someone looking for work. He thought about it a lot and now was the time to hire a girl or woman to stay with Louise during her last month of her condition and perhaps some time after.

During the winter, the stable wasn't as busy so James could spend more time at home. The winter months passed with the new minister taking the lead at Christmas. It was such a relief for James and Louise. Louise continued to feel tired and saw the doctor every time she could. She watched the weather as she took care of Betty, thinking how glad she was that they were in town especially in her condition. She played the piano at church but asked James if they could bring it home, because she wanted to play and start teaching Betty as soon as possible. He promised and between the minister and a few friends they accomplished that. Louise found a lot of comfort in playing and often at night James would join her singing hymns. It often put the baby to sleep listening to the music.

The winter passed and the town was beginning to show signs of more people coming by wagons when the weather showed the welcome signs of spring. Even James and Betty enjoyed a little walk in the slush although Louise refused for fear of slipping and falling. The doctor insisted she slow down or get some help, but she said they were doing just that. Now that they were in town, Louise did not have a garden to worry about or cutting hair. However, those were two of the things that she really enjoyed doing and missed it. She was kept busy with Betty and could walk over to Liz's for a chat besides sewing and cleaning.

Time was going by and the hot weeks of summer didn't make Louise feel any better. She thought the sun was turning the country brown. Rain was more than welcome.

Then one day James arrived home from work to find Louise laying down, and crying. Betty was in her crib and crying as well. He quickly, shed his coat and boots, and took Betty in his arms, and sat down beside Louise on the bed.

"My labor pains have started, and the doctor is not here at the moment. He might not be able to travel. It is early, so I am worried, is all," she sighed slowly taking a big breath and closing her eyes. She looked like she was going to sleep. James was beside himself. Just at that moment, he heard the door open and close and when he came out to see who it was, he was surprised to see Meg standing there, covered in snow.

"What in the world, are you doing here?" he asked

"I guess, James, I was fretting so much, John, told me to ride into town and check on Louise. I was worried about her since the last time we chatted and it looks like, I am needed here,"

"My dear girl, I have never been so glad to see anyone, in my life. Louise is in labor; I don't know any more than that. She has looked terribly tired of late, but never complains. Please go and check on her. I will put the kettle on and look after Betty," James was in tears as he spoke.

Meg quickly got to work, and checking on Louise, found her resting, though she started to cry.

"I am afraid, I might be wrong in my due date, Meg,"

"No problem, we will take care of you until the doctor arrives and if he doesn't, I know what to do," she said while, straightening the blankets and pillows.

"Don't worry James, but you should take Betty to Liz's. She might get scared if her mom starts to cry or holler," she told him putting the kettle on, that he had forgotten.

Meg was quite at home in the house she once she lived in. While she was getting some towels out, Lorette came through the door.

"I saw you last Sunday and you expressed your concerns about Louise. I saw the lights on here and my husband told me to check it out, knowing I wouldn't rest. I have some training as a midwife, so if I can help in anyway," she said quickly, removing her coat, while James left with a bundled up Betty. He only nodded as they passed. He was only too glad to get out of the way. He knew that these women were comfortable with this event, but he was still worried about his Louise. He would say a prayer for her. He was welcomed at Liz's and she was only too pleased to look after Betty for a while. Liz made a bed for them and Betty went to sleep but James laid there and prayed.

"Please let me know, what is happening? If you need Bill for anything, he is just sitting around bored," said Liz when she realized James was wide awake in the early morning.

"If Bill could come with me, I would appreciate it. I need to check on the horses and I might be needed at home at some time. I am really worried about Louise," he said with a tear running down his cheek.

"Bill," she hollered, "you are needed,"

Bill was only too happy to accompany James. He quickly donned his coat and boots and both took off into the wind. The wind seemed to be picking up and gusting at times. They quickly went to the stables, where horses needed some attention. Both men set to work, getting water and feed for the horses. Thank goodness there were only three.

"The minister and his wife are just what we needed, I believe," he said, but James head was bowed in prayer, so Bill didn't say anymore. He felt the area owed this man a great deal and he also knew how devout he was and how he loved his wife and daughter. He then also bowed his head and said a quick prayer. Louise would be such a loss to the community. She was such a talented and kind woman, he thought as he went about cleaning the stalls.

Back at the house, the labor pains continued. There was no doubt that Louise was going to deliver a baby somewhat early. The women waited and prayed, watching her closely. When Bill and James stopped in and Bill saw James distress, he suggested he come back to their place for awhile. Betty would be there so it might be a good idea. James thought about it for a moment and agreed. He couldn't bear the moans that were coming from their bedroom.

Later, found James fast asleep beside Betty on one of the beds. Some one had covered them with a quilt, so they were toasty warm and the wind had gradually calmed. At James house, all was quiet at the moment, both Meg and Lorette sat trying desperately to stay awake, when the door suddenly opened and Dr. Taylor walked in holding onto his hat. He looked cold. The women came alive and quickly, took his coat and hat and sat him down. One took his boots off and the other rubbed his hands and arms. He looked at the women with appreciation in his eyes. He spoke haltingly.

"It's been a wild ride to get here. Thank goodness my horse seemed to know the way, because at times I couldn't see anything for the wind and rain. How is our patient?"

"She's asleep now, poor thing just played out. The labor seems to have stopped," said Lorette, who introduced herself, when the doctor looked at her questioningly.

"Okay, do you think it is false labor?"

"No, actually, I don't. The pains are strong," she answered and a long moan came from the bedroom alerting them. They ran to the bedroom, as she screamed again.

"Okay, time the pains, and let's prepare for a delivery. She might be having some difficulty. Where is James?" he asked suddenly realizing he wasn't there.

"He's over at Liz's, where Betty is. He hasn't come back, so maybe he's fallen asleep. He looked mighty tired," said Meg.

"Okay, good I don't have two patients, let's concentrate on Louise,"

Two hours later, she did deliver a very small baby girl, and although she was small, she had a very loud cry. Louise fell asleep almost immediately, simply played out.

"Take care of the baby, will you, Lorette?"

"Meg, perhaps, you can help me clean up our patient? We will make her comfortable, then I will wake her to welcome her brand new baby," said Dr. Taylor.

"I will put the kettle on as well," replied Meg. "And when we are finished, I am going to run over to Liz's to get James. He will be so relieved and will want to see them as soon as possible."

As they talked, Louise, woke up and demanded to see her baby.

"Okay, my lady, she will be with you in a moment, she is being bathed and wrapped. She is a beautiful little girl. Congratulations!" answered the doctor.

"Oh, where is James?" answered Louise smiling.

"Be here shortly," replied Meg as she donned her coat. She would hurry over to Liz's. The wind had calmed down and was merely gusting occasionally, so she didn't have much trouble walking there. When she got there, she banged on the door loudly, bringing Bill on the double. He looked at her frowning, "What is it? Is something wrong? James is asleep beside Betty. Do you want me to wake him?"

"Yes, he is the father of a beautiful baby girl," she said excitedly.

"Oh my," said Liz, hearing the commotion and so did James who came out of the bedroom in a hurry asking, "What did you say?"

"Get your coat, your wife and daughter are waiting for you," answered Meg.

"Leave Betty here, it is too nasty out for her at this time. I will bring her over later. Louise needs you, so go," called Liz

There was jubilation for the next few hours. Dr. Taylor was tired and requested a place to lay down. Meg showed him to a bed in Betty's room, where James had already placed a single bed beside the crib. The Doctor was asleep in minutes while the others were too excited to rest and sat at the table with a cup of tea while James talked to Louise. Louise had already decided on a name for her baby and James agreed on it being 'Florence'. The baby was snuggled beside Louise and looked so pretty that James decided to leave them rest and joined the women. Meg declared she would stay and take care of mother and baby while needed, then perhaps Lorette could come and help out. The doctor of course, would check them on them before he left. He was staying at Liz's. He usually has more patients when he comes, and of course, Meg was one of them. They were so surprised but pleased that he came out in this weather.

"God Bless him and my girls," said James smiling broadly.

A tired group slept soundlessly, some in chairs and some in beds. The day was sunny with no wind. James groaned when he looked outside. This was going to be a rough day for all. He talked to the women, who assured him they would take care of mother and baby for as long as was necessary. He assured them that he had hired a girl to help Louise during the day, but not for babysitting, although he thought she might be quite capable. Lorette let him know that she would be around as well. Satisfied he went off to work knowing all was taken care of. He was so relieved and bowed his head in prayer as he trudged to work. There should not be much action today, he thought, but who knows.

It wasn't long before Louise was up and around, as busy as ever. It was as if, she never lost a day, except that the baby gleaned a lot of her attention now and Betty was proving to be wanting attention as well. It was a trying time for all, but she had lots of help and was so appreciative of it and said so.

The days went by. Meg had returned home as soon as she thought everything was fine. John had driven in with several farmers needing supplies and followed her home.

Lorette came over often, and helped both with the children and Louise, assisting and making Louise rest often. They became good friends and her husband often joined them at night to chat. He and James were engaged in many a discussion on the Bible and both seemed to enjoy the camaraderie. Then one night James approached the minister about baptism, because he wanted his girls to be christened. He told him that Louise had already made dresses for the occasion, to the delight of both the minister and his wife.

"Why yes, I would like to do that very much," said Rev. Evans and I daresay there might even be more parents wanting their children to be christened. I will request it at the next service. And by the way, I am going to visit some more people, as soon as I can or as soon as the weather will permit," he added smiling.

James and Louise were well satisfied with their decision and welcomed the idea of other children being christened as well.

As time went by more people were out and about. There was again a lot of building going on and the saloon was busy all the time. Saturday nights, bothered James. He did not approve of all the shouting and goings on there. He was not an advocate of Saturday night dances at the school house as well, and he let everyone know it.

In the meantime, since the piano was at home, Louise expressed a desire to start teaching the children and perhaps others. James thought about it a lot. They both liked music and he wanted their girls to be able to play especially the hymns that he loved. He would join them on the trombone.

As Betty grew, Louise started her on the piano. She was a natural but the baby Florence, was still too young. She vowed to work with her when she got older.

As time went by, James continued to work at the stables, venting frequently about the heathens about. People came and most of them left, after one harsh winter. Those that stayed were hardy people and the demand for supplies increased bringing more businesses.

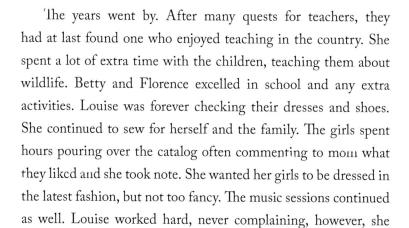

The years went by. After many quests for teachers, they had at last found one who enjoyed teaching in the country. She spent a lot of extra time with the children, teaching them about wildlife. Betty and Florence excelled in school and any extra activities. Louise was forever checking their dresses and shoes. She continued to sew for herself and the family. The girls spent hours pouring over the catalog often commenting to mom what they liked and she took note. She wanted her girls to be dressed in the latest fashion, but not too fancy. The music sessions continued as well. Louise worked hard, never complaining, however, she was slowing down. She seemed to be having problems. James often found her laying down in the middle of the day claiming to be just resting. However, he noticed dark circles under her eyes and knew she was worried. When he approached her about it, she would claim it was just rest she needed.

However, James mentioned it to the doctor who now had an office in town and an assistant to look after his patients. The next time the doctor met Louise, he stopped to talk to her and noticed the same as James.

"Come along to my office," he told her.

"Whatever for?" she answered.

"You are looking a bit run down, Louise, and I am wondering why, that's all?"

"All right, I am not feeling up to par, but I was just putting it down to age," she said innocently.

After talking to her for sometime, he discovered, she was worrying about the pains she sometimes had and that maybe her kidneys were not working. When she said that, the doctor became alarmed. She was sick and would not admit it.

"Louise, I would like you to go into the hospital in Saskatoon. That way we can give you some tests and make sure everything is all right?"

"Oh, I don't know. I have to think about the girls and James. What would he do?"

"Louise, if he lost you, what do you think he would do?"

"Let me talk to him?"

"Fine, but I need to know tonight," he answered her with urgency in his voice.

She promised and left, worry lines on her brow. She could not fathom leaving her family for anytime but she also felt, she must get to the bottom of those pains and the problems she was having. It was something she did not like talking about, even to James. Going to the out house was becoming a problem as the pains were becoming stronger.

The day after she talked to the doctor, she collapsed and James found her on the floor.

Immediately, he went for the doctor and between them they got her on the bed. She woke up very disoriented. The decision to go to the hospital was made. They would leave as soon as James could find help to look after the two girls, who were at school. Lorette answered James call for help.

Chapter Fourteen

Hospital Visit

The trip to Saskatoon would take some time. He loaned a buggy and horse and made the buggy as comfortable as possible, filling it with hay and covering it with a blanket. The doctor and James made Louise as comfortable as possible and left with a promise to get word back as soon as possible.

The trip was long and hard on Louise, but she said very little, often closing her eyes as if she was asleep. She could not however disguise her feelings. Every time, the buggy hit a rough spot, she gave out an elongated moan and closed her eyes in prayer as did James. It took them –twenty-four hours changing horses halfway, where there was a dwelling with caretakers that traveller's used, called a 'halfway house'.

They were exhausted when they stopped in front of that house. A woman came out to meet them nodding a greeting and realizing that they had a sick patient, took charge, ushering them inside and mouthing to her husband to take care of the horses. They were only too glad to let someone else take care of Louise. With the help of the doctor she was immediately put to bed and offered a drink or something to eat, but refused. James and the doctor, however, did have some tea and stew and then begged to be excused and were offered a bed each.

Early next morning they left after eating, paying and moving Louise carefully back into the buggy. She moaned as they helped her, but motioned to keep going. The lady of the house, spoke then saying, "She is a very strong woman. God be with you," and waved to them as they prompted the horse to run.

They made good time and finally saw a mass of houses which was their destination. The hospital was a large square, white washed building, with a wide entrance. As they drove up, they were met by nurses and a couple of men in white. Louise was admitted immediately. Dr. Taylor went on ahead of James and was explaining to the doctor in charge, the problem. After tying up the horses, James was beside himself, not knowing what to do, when a nurse guided him into a room and told him to sit down and the doctors would talk to him soon. She brought him a cup of tea, which he appreciated. He sighed and closed his eyes again in prayer. Tears streamed down his cheeks, as he sat there. After what seemed like a very long time, a doctor came in to talk to him.

"James, we are going to keep Louise here for a few days to do some tests. She is not in any danger that we can tell right now. You can see her now. The nurse will show you the way. Then I believe you need to get some rest"

"Thanks, I will go see her before I look for a place to stay the night.""

Little did he know, Dr. Taylor had ordered the horse and buggy taken care of when they came in and asked the attendants to look after James and that he liked tea.

When he saw Louise, he tried hard to be strong, but seeing her so white faced in bed, he couldn't help but get emotional.

"I am sorry James, the pain was so strong today, I didn't mean for you to worry," she said quietly.

"Don't worry about me, just get well. I don't know what I would do without you, my love. I am staying the night and we will see what happens tomorrow. I will be back later. My prayers are with you." he said haltingly.

Two days went by, and there seemed to be no diagnosis. James decided to go home. He needed to see the girls. He went to Louise and told her what he planned. He wanted to bring the girls in to see her but she said no and told him to wait a few days before you do that. Perhaps I will be better by then and that is what they decided to do.

He rode horseback home, stopping at the same house half-way for a rest and food.

The girls were glad to see him and were beside themselves wondering what had happened. After greeting them, he noted that Betty immediately sat at the piano for a long time. James thought perhaps it was relieving some of her tension. He also noted that she was an excellent player and somehow had he missed that, or hadn't he been listening. Florence sat close to him, with a sad look on her face. She was the one that came running when he drove up and threw herself into his arms crying. Betty came out of the house too, but was very serene. She too looked sad and inquired about Mom more than once. He was proud of his girls. They helped around the house and when he spoke to Lorette, she praised the two.

He spoke softly to the girls. They listened intently and expressed a desire to go see their mother. James said he would think about it. He would have to make arrangements at both ends. However, he thought maybe it would be best for the girl's sake and he did not know how long Louise would be in hospital anyway. Hopefully not long, he thought sighing, at that point he decided to go to the stable and talk to his assistant and make some arrangements. He would have to talk to Lorette as well, but before he could do anything, Liz and Bill were at the door with questions. Of course, they had heard, it was a small town.

"James, do what you have to do. We will look after the girls if you wish or your work and will let the people know at church. They will pray for her, I know," said Liz and Bill nodded as well.

"We owe so much to you and Louise, and I feel so helpless right now. Let me do your job for a while until things settle down?" Bill offered.

"Good, I am going to take the girls in to see her, not tomorrow but the next day. Perhaps they will know what is wrong by then," answered James.

When they left, Bill spoke up softly, "He looks so forlorn, my heart goes out to him and those girls,"

"I know; I too feel helpless. I am not usually a praying person, but at this point I am going to be," added Liz.

It was decided to go the next day. He told Bill, who was going to work for him and Lorette indicated she was willing to check on the house while he was gone. The girls were excited and told to pack a few over night clothes, because they would have to stay overnight on the way and in Saskatoon. It would be a long ride so they must be strong and patient. He organized the horse and buggy on loan and by night had everything under control. Liz came over to tell him, she would be packing a lunch for them on the way and would bring it over in the morning. James was so appreciative and told her so.

The trip started out uneventful, but by lunch time, the girls were getting impatient, so he decided to stop, rest the horses and have their lunch. Florence remarked that that was a very good idea. Just like her mother, thought James, smiling. They found a nice sunny spot that looked like it had been a stopping place for others. They tied up the horse and James went to work watering it, while the girls, took the lunch and set it out in the back of the buggy, standing to drink their tea and eat their biscuits filled with meat of some kind, but commenting on how good it was. There was cake and cookies.

"What a feast," exclaimed Florence, looking at her Dad, who winked at her. Betty, however, ate in silence. James sensed the girl was fretting.

"You will soon see your mother, Betty. Will that make you feel better?" asked James

"Maybe," she answered quietly. There were so smiles, no enthusiasm at all. All this made James worry.

Soon they were back on the road. The horse was rested and ready to run. He had waited patiently while the girls ate but wasn't hungry. At their next stop, they would stop and rest. They would have a chance to sleep on a bed. He had brought blankets along, just in case. *It would do the girls good and I need to rest. We still have a way to go tomorrow before we reach Saskatoon.*

When they reached the half-way stop, both girls were fast asleep. He didn't like to wake them, but he had no choice. He had to rest, feed and water the horse. The trip was taking its toll on all of them. One by one they woke up and slowly got down from the buggy. Florence made so bones about being tired.

The girls looked carefully at the stopping place. Noting it was a gray two story house with a small porch in front, and windows on either side. A small woman, with coal black hair pulled back in a bun at the back of her neck, stood on the steps, smiling. She greeted them and asked them in. I will make you something to eat and show you young ladies to a bed upstairs and your father can sleep down stairs. Both girls stared at her and looked at the small kitchen and the large table covered with a colored cloth and white china plates and cups. They were mesmerized and looked at everything not saying a word.

There was benches on either side of the table and two big chairs in the room off the kitchen, which held a large stove and another narrow table with shelves above. The wall in the big room was covered with flowered paper, which Florence found fascinating. Betty followed her hand when she pointed, saying, how pretty it was. But Florence was the only one to show her enthusiasm. James thanked the lady, who introduced herself as Mrs. West. She was very agile and happily went about the small kitchen, humming. She was dressed the same as Louise, skirt to the floor, long sleeves and a high neckline. All this resonated with James for she reminded him of the women in his church back home. She was ruddy cheeked and dark eyed with such a happy countenance that he hadn't noticed before.

"Now girls, we can all rest here. This lady will see to you. I am going to see to the horse and then I will join you for something to eat and then we will try and sleep. Tomorrow you will be able to see your Mother,"

"Thanks Dad, I hope and pray she is all right," replied Betty somberly.

He knew then how deep she was worrying. So in spite of his own worry, he had to show the poor girl, some help. Aw, he knew what to do.

"Let all of us say a prayer now. First you Florence, then Betty and then myself,"

They were obedient girls and bowed their heads. "I pray that Mama will be better, and I know God is looking after her," said Florence followed by Betty.

"I pray that she will be up and about soon, because I miss her so," she said crying suddenly. James moved over and held her little body. She was sobbing so much her body seemed to convulse. As he held her, he continued with his own prayer,

"I pray that your Mother does get well and with God's help come home to us soon," as he spoke he too cried. Mrs. West looked on knowingly and waited for them to settle down.

Before he went to see to his horse, Mr. West came in and gestured to him that the horse was taken care of and that he need not worry. Mrs. West was very efficient and took care of the girls as soon as they finished eating. She was surprised when the girls

requested some water to wash and did so. Florence smiled as she
pointed to the pretty bed spread and pillows to match. There
was only a bed and a wash stand and a table in the bedroom, but
the girls said nothing after looking around. Mrs. West watched
as they knelt down to pray, change and get into bed. They were
soon fast asleep. Mrs. West returned to the kitchen and motioned
to James to follow her to his quarters. He was appreciative and
showed it, but was eager to lay down. He too was soon sound
asleep.

Morning dawned bright and sunny. He was abruptly
awakened by the girls. They were washed and dressed and ready
to go. He would have to hurry along because they were becoming
impatient. While the girls waited, they wandered to the windows
to look outside. Florence discovered the chicken pen and laughed
out loud as she watched the rooster crow.

"Oh, Mrs. West is that your son out there with the chickens?"

"Oh my," Mrs. West said as she hurried out the door and
around the house to the pen.

Watching, the girls, couldn't believe what they saw. She was
bringing the young boy into the house, by his ear. He was crying.
Both girls were awe struck and watched with their father who
motioned to the girls to be quiet.

"You have been stealing my eggs?" said Mrs. West.

"Only two," he stuttered.

"None before?" she asked.

"No, tomorrow is my birthday and Mama couldn't bake a
cake for me because she has no eggs. I thought that I could just
borrow two for her,"

"Why didn't you just ask me, young man?"

"I don't know you and the kids at school say you are tough," he kept blubbering. Mrs. West was studying him closely.

"You live about a mile from here. Don't you? Well, I tell you what. If you come tomorrow after school and help me with the chickens, that will pay for the eggs you took today. And if you would like to work for me another day, I will give you another two eggs,"

He was about 8 yrs. old, short and chubby with blond curly hair that was unruly and a face that exuded innocence. He hadn't noticed the girls before, but when he did, his face went beet red and he looked away. He looked back at Mrs. West with awe, as if he couldn't believe what she was saying.

"I ccan ddo tthat," he said hurriedly and cupping the eggs carefully he rushed to the door and ran as fast as he could away from the house.

James was fascinated at what just transpired and asked her, "Has someone been stealing your eggs?"

"Yes, I thought it was a crow or something like that, but there was never any shell left so then I knew that it had human qualities," she replied.

"Before we leave, I would like to pay you for our stay. It has been most pleasant. We will be returning in a day or so and will probably stop over again on our way home. I understand the girls told you what happened and why their mother is in hospital," James told her.

"Then pay me when you return. I look forward to visiting the girls. I don't have any children of my own and I enjoy talking to them. They are extremely well-behaved girls and both so different. You must be proud. I also pray your wife will get better," she answered with a smile. Then added, "my husband has your horse and buggy waiting for you."

James hadn't noticed his horse and buggy pull up in front, but thanked her.

"Come on, girls, let's be off. We have taken up enough of Mrs. West time. Please say goodbye and thank her,"

Both girls quickly thanked her and ran to the buggy. They were anxious to get going too. The day passed uneventfully as they rode along. The girls did talk about that young boy and wondered about the chickens. It kept them occupied for most of the time. James had already inquired about a stable and had instructions where to go and what to do. When they arrived, he sent the girls to wait inside until he stabled the horse. They were eager to do it and jumped off and ran inside as soon as he stopped. Inside, the girls were in awe. They had never been in a hospital before. As they looked around and were amazed to find their mother, sitting there and ran to her with outstretched arms. Both were so happy. Louise hugged the two and laughed wiping their tears.

"Can you come home, Mama?" inquired Florence.

"I believe so," Louise replied smiling.

"Oh how happy father is going to be," quipped Betty, sounding so grown-up

When James came through the door, he couldn't believe what he saw. Both girl's ran to him and declared, "Mama is coming home,"

"Wonderful, but," said James as he gazed at Louise, who nodded and smiled.

"I feel much better. The pains have subsided and the doctor has given me some instructions and medicine, I guess you could call it,"

James spoke up then, "I can't take you home tonight though, Louise. We will have to stay because it is a long trip and it is late."

"Perhaps, we could go half way and stay at Mrs. West house. She is such a nice person," said Louise.

"No, Louise, that is not possible. I am tired, my horse is tired and the girls might think they are not, but I know better. And besides you have just gotten out of bed, what are you thinking. I cannot be responsible for all of you," he said slowly with a tear running down his cheek. Adding, "I want to take you home more than anything, but I must rest, my love,"

"It's okay Mama, we can wait until tomorrow and it will be fun, right Betty?"," replied Florence again in that big girl voice. She hugged her Mother again and again.

A doctor suddenly appeared and saw the anxious girls, and spoke up, "What a lovely family you have Louise. However, I must insist that you stay one more night. Tomorrow I will discharge you. Now back to bed!" he said as he pointed to a nurse. That settled it. The girls were ecstatic and let James know. He too, was looking forward to taking them all home. They fairly bounced around him as they left for the rooming house he had booked for them.

The following day dawned sunny but cool, with a slight breeze. James was anxious to get going, now they were rested. They bundled Louise up in blankets, to sit in the front seat and the girls cuddled up together in the box behind. Their horse was ready to run and James gave it the opportunity to do so. The

buggy bumped and swayed along. Since they had seen the scenery
the girls just ignored it and chatted for a little while, but soon
fell asleep. James and Louise also chatted for a while, but James
explained he wanted to concentrate on the road, which was rutted
and there were wagons passing. He waved but did not stop.

After some hours, they arrived at the halfway House. Both
girls rushed to help Louise, who was tired and happy to allow
them. James waited, but Mr. West was out front and took the
horse by the rein, motioning James to follow the rest. He never
spoke. Mrs. West remained on the steps and waved the family
inside. She made several gestures to her husband, before following.

Inside Florence was excited to show her Mother the rooms.
She pointed to the table with its floral decorated shiny oilcloth
and the papered walls, also with a floral design in a large room.
Betty just tagged along hanging on to Louise' arm.

"Sit thee down, please, and I will get you some tea," exclaimed
Mrs. West smiling broadly at Florence.

"Thank you," said all of them in unison and then laughed.
Florence kept looking through the window at the chicken pen, as
if looking for someone. Mrs. West realized that and told her that
the boy was there today and was so happy. He said he would be
back again.

"Oh," cried Florence who then proceeded to tell her Mother
the story, leaving nothing out. She motioned to her Mother to
come look out the window at the chicken pen.

Soon James noticed Louise yawning and suggested that they
should get some rest. While they were talking, Mr. West came in
and nodded to the group. Mrs. West told them then that he was
deaf and motioned to him to join them at the table. He smiled

and pointed to the girls. The girls realizing, he was meaning them, smiled and Florence rushed over and shook his hand. He was so flattered that he stood up and bowed to her. A little later when they retired Florence said, "Mama, you should see the water pitcher, Mrs. West, brought us. It is beautiful and you should see the bed blanket," as they were being ushered to the bedroom upstairs.

Florence was so enamored by it all, it made Louise smile. Before James rested however he wanted to thank Mr. West and explained that to his wife. In turn she motioned to him and he smiled and nodded to James.

"I will pay you in the morning," he said to them.

"That will be fine, now go to bed and rest. We will see you in the morning, early," Mrs. West answered.

James' brow was furrowed as he laid down because he hadn't noticed a barn. There must be a stable or something. I must have been tired for I didn't notice anything that Florence was talking about at all. When he thought about it, he wondered if Dr. Taylor paid them on our first stay. Thinking of that he fell fast asleep as soon as he prayed and laid down. He did remember to look around in the morning and found that indeed there was a stable almost hidden behind the house and attached to the chicken pen. How come I didn't notice that James wondered. Was I blind?

He did not have to arouse the girls or Louise, because they were already dressed and were enjoying breakfast and chatting away to Mrs. West, when he looked out from his small room. Florence was so excited telling her mother everything about the place and Louise just followed her hands that pointed, smiling.

While James was paying Mrs. West, Mr. West had brought the horse and buggy to the steps, awaiting the little family. He smiled broadly at the girls and bowed to Florence and assisted her into the buggy. As soon as they were sitting, James hawed and they were off. They made many stops along the way, just to rest the horse. They all fell asleep except James. There was nothing much to see anyway, declared Betty, when James asked her.

"Well, there is the odd rabbit, hawk, deer, prairie chicken, song birds in the tall reeds," he exclaimed. He was trying hard to make the trip more enjoyable. But as Florence pointed out, there are no trees or bushes for them to nest or hide. She made a point, thought Louise who never said anything, just nodded in agreement.

They arrived home tired but happy. Bill was there to take the horse and buggy and Liz and Lorette were there to settle the little family.

"Thank you," was said in unison again. They all laughed and were told to go right to bed and they would all see them the morrow. Liz and Lorette were there early next morning with the intention of making breakfast and helping them get organized for the day.

As the days passed, Louise regained her strength and began sewing and doing all her housework herself. She was back to her old self, humming and enjoying her family. She had found that if she took the doctors advise and took one teaspoon of mineral oil every morning and watched what she ate, she had no more problems.

Chapter Fifteen

The Girls

The years went by. The girls were growing up and a big help to Louise. She was teaching them, cooking and music. Neither girl was interested in sewing, which was a disappointment to Louise. However, Betty made up for it in music. The girl was excelling, to be sure. She was becoming popular among the church people and the local young people. Louise realized she was extremely pretty with her dark curly hair, striking dark eyes and light complexion, hoping it would not deter her from a career in music. She had enrolled her in music lessons through the mail.

Betty's ability to read music amazed Louise. She would sit and play after school. Florence on the other hand, was a great housekeeper and a fun person to be with. She often caused them to laugh almost to tears. She was also very popular. She was not quite as pretty as Betty, but she had an endearing character, one that you just could not resist. Florence had brown hair with a rounder face and darker complexion. Both girls were very close and did a lot together. Betty might have been popular but she always included Florence. And that's perhaps one reason that the two of them got into trouble with their father.

The town held dances at the school house every Saturday night. Betty had been asked many times if she would play with the band. Both girls knew that their father would be strongly against it. However, like teenagers, they wanted to go so badly they devised a plan.

At bedtime, they would obediently go to bed, wait a while, until they thought mother and father wouldn't be paying any attention to them, then execute their plan. They managed to get the upstairs window open and quietly climbed down a pre-set ladder. They ran to the school house where a dance was in full swing. As soon as they arrived, the band called Betty to play and she quickly sat down at the piano. She was happily doing just that when James appeared at the door. He walked through the gawking dancers and grabbed Betty by the arm, pulling her outside. She screamed and Florence followed trying to stop her father. She tried to talk to him but he pushed her aside and smacked Betty on the backside, while pointing towards home oblivious to the people who ran beside, begging for the girls. There was nothing they could do. James anger and obsession with 'sin' had taken over his brain. There was no consolation!

"Home now, and if I ever catch you doing that again, I don't know what my actions might be," he said as he proceeded to hit Betty across the backside again and again. He was mad beyond reason and the girls knew it. They had broken his trust.

Louise met them at the door, with tears running down her face. She begged James to quit hitting them and quickly drew them behind her motioning to him to sit down. She pointed upstairs to the girls, who were crying and shaking. Quietly they went and Louise put the kettle on and sat down in front of James. She was very angry and it showed. James bowed his head, closed his eyes and started praying quietly for quite some time, while Louise sat fingering a cup of tea.

Finally, it was the time to speak and that she did with a ferocity that James had never seen. She never let up until he looked up at her with such misery on his face. He uttered, "Dear, God, I lost my temper and I feel horrible, because that is not what I should have done. I pray for forgiveness from you, my girls and my God."

Louise finally went to see to the girls. She hugged and cried with them. It was going to be a long night. Eventually the girls cried themselves to sleep and Louise checked on James, who was still sitting, praying. She noted his eyes were red and swollen and walked over and held him for a very long time. It was morning when they finally went to bed. James would be late for work, but he did not care for once.

The next day, Louise noticed that Betty was limping but didn't complain or eat much and went back to the bedroom for some time. When Louise went to check, she was crying and that's when she noticed the bruises on her leg. Checking further she found large bruises on her backside. The girl was in pain. Louise realized only time would help but the pain would last a very long time, even after the bruises healed. She prayed that the girls would forgive their father but knew in her heart, this would have a lasting effect.

The girls never forgot and both vowed that as soon as they were old enough, they would leave Lashburn. It was a promise they made to each other that night after the humiliation they had endured. They often cried and chatted to one another before they could sleep. Betty was hurt physically and mentally and it would remain with her forever.

The girls continued to do their chores and help their mother, but their heart was not in it as before. Florence, lost her exuberance, but continued to obey all instructions, including praying and reading the Bible. Betty began planning that very night to leave Lashburn, as soon as she was eighteen and would help Florence when she turned eighteen. They never ventured out again and quietly minded their parents, but Louise knew that had been a turning point in their relationship with their father. It was like an unseen cloud that existed over the family. Both girls would eventually leave. She could not blame them, there was a big world to explore and she would worry but understand, just as she had.

Not only had she noted her girls change but the whole town was changing. There were more people coming in, setting up businesses and the stable although it had been a crucial part of town at one time was not so now. The minister and his wife remained for some years but had recently moved on where upon they were waiting for another one.

Meg and John came in to visit with their two children. They only heard once from the Taylor children in Scotland, but Meg kept on hoping. They were doing very well on the farm and had expanded. Bill and Liz had retired. Bill expressed a desire to go to the Coast, where the weather was more like England and that's what they planned. The girls often talked to Bill and Liz and told them of their plans, and Liz realized they had not said anything to their parents, so they kept quiet. Bill told them they would always be welcome at their home, when they moved.

Epilogue

The year 1925, saw many changes in and around the country. Betty excelled in music and continued taking music lessons by mail from Toronto Conservatory. James knew that he had lost the trust of his girls, but although he apologized often, he realized the spark was gone. Louise had given him a talking to that night so long ago, that he would never forget. It was the one time; she spoke with such ferocity. He remembered sitting and praying all night – that night. He knew too that he would never forget it.

During the fall, Betty turned eighteen, she expressed a desire to go to Vancouver to continue her studies in music. He had no choice but to let her go. He would try just once more to apologize and wish her well. Louise asked her to please keep in touch. You are so precious to both of us she explained. Your father loves you very much.

Betty was becoming a very independent young lady. She made friends easily and after finishing school started working while helping at home. Neither girl ventured out again unless James and Louise okayed it. It took some time but Betty soon had the money she needed and more. She confided in Louise her plan to take the bus to Vancouver and that she had written to Liz for permission to stay with them in New Westminster. They had written back and expressed a delight at having her.

Florence cried when she saw her packing, but they had made a pact and Betty told her that as soon as she was ready, she was to earn enough money to take the bus to Vancouver as well and she could stay with her. By that time, she should have her own place to live.

It was Florence that simply flew into packing and cleaning, washing, ironing and above all keeping the conversation lively, once again as she made her plans. She worked part time after school during her last years and even helped in the diner. As soon as she had more than enough money for bus fare and some extra, she told her mother she was ready to go.

When Florence joined Betty, she found work as well and both girls enjoyed doing things together especially the night life. However, they often expressed how they missed their parents and wished they would move closer.

Within these years, Betty built up a reputation as a pianist and was in demand to play for weddings, funerals, cantatas, plays, and anywhere that a pianist was needed with the exception of dance bands. Both girls wrote often to her Mother and Dad about the weather being so much easier and how jobs were plentiful and how they wished they would join them.

When James read the letters, he knew in his heart, that Louise would love to move near the girls and he too would enjoy the weather, the way they pictured it. It would take some doing but, yes, it was time to move on. He hated to leave the people he knew, the farmers and the business men and women that worked so hard, but he also had to think of Louise, the love of his life. And he too missed the girls. He would make it up to Betty if it took him the rest of his life.

Louise wrote to the girls to let them know what they were planning, telling them that it would take some time but that she was looking forward to coming to the Coast and the English weather.

When Betty and Florence got the news, they were elated. They also knew that it was going to be a bit of a shock. People were wearing different styles of clothing. No more covering the ankles, wrists and neck. There were changes going on everywhere. They often talked about what father would think about the changes in apparel but also knew their mother would absorb it without question.

James, in the meantime, gave his notice at the stables, although he knew they were doomed seeing the odd car coming. People would soon look at better transportation. He knew that horses were becoming a thing of the past witnessing some of John's farming machinery. Another era disappearing. However, he also knew, the people were strong and there was still the need for spiritual guidance and schooling even with the many changes coming. He had talked to John and Meg about it when they visited. They talked about their plans and vowed to keep in touch.

Louise expressed the fact that though she was excited at being near the girls, she felt sad at saying goodbye to so many friends.

The days seemed to fly by as they planned their move. The furniture they kept was sent on by train. Some they left behind and some they discarded or sold. Now all they had to do was get their bus tickets and say goodbye to Saskatchewan, a part of their history that would be locked in their memory forever.

Thank you for completing *Leeds to Lashburn.*

We would love if you could help by posting a review at your book retailer and on the PageMaster Publishing site. It only takes a minute and it would really help others by giving them an idea of your experience.

Thanks

Find Joyce Sjogren on the Pagemaster store:
https://pagemasterpublishing.ca/by/joyce-sjogren/

To order more copies of this book, find books by other Canadian authors, or make inquiries about publishing your own book, contact PageMaster at:

PageMaster Publication Services Inc.
11340-120 Street, Edmonton, AB T5G 0W5
books@pagemaster.ca
780-425-9303

catalogue and e-commerce store
PageMasterPublishing.ca/Shop

About the author:

Joyce has written many short stories, some published in a local newspaper and some she made into a book called 'Wildlife Drama'. She has entered and won prizes in fairs in Central Alberta and a Silver Medal in the Alberta Seniors Games for a true story on sibling rivalry. This is her first attempt at a novel which is her way of leaving a legacy of ancestral history and the untold hardships that the grandparents encountered when they immigrated.